THREE BALCONIES

STORIES AND A NOVELLA

Bruce Jay Friedman

THREE BALCONIES

STORIES AND A NOVELLA

BIBLIOASIS

FIRST EDITION

Library and Archives Canada Cataloguing in Publication

Friedman, Bruce Jay, 1930-
        Three balconies : stories and a novella / Bruce Jay Friedman.

ISBN 10: 1-897231-45-8
ISBN 13: 978-1-897231-45-6

        I. Title.

PS3556.R5T47 2008   813'.54   C2008-904000-7

Jacket iStockphoto: "Cartagena Balconies"
        © Menso van Westrhenen

PRINTED AND BOUND IN THE USA

For Pat and Molly

Contents

The Secret Man

HERBERT PLOTKIN did not so much appear in Jacob's new neighborhood as he seemed to loom up out of nowhere. He didn't look a bit like his name. He was tall and blonde and had Nordic features. His body was as tightly carved as if he had been in prison. Though he disappeared into a good building at night, no one had ever seen his parents. There was some talk that he was adopted – a disgrace at the time – but you did not dare say it.

He took up a position in front of the neighborhood drugstore each day and used it as a guard post. Sweeping his hands back through his luxuriant hair, he peered out at the streets and monitored the traffic in all directions. There didn't seem to be any way to go anywhere or do anything without passing before him.

Jacob was afraid of Plotkin and spent seven years of his life trying not to show it.

It had begun as a happy time. Jacob's father, who worked in New York City's garment center, had gotten a raise. The extra money enabled Jacob and his parents to move into a new building with a white brick exterior and an elevator. The apartment was smaller than their old one, but it was fresh and cheery and had a step-down living room. His parents had bought an imitation fireplace with a radio built into the side of it. With a bowl of fruit in his lap, Jacob would lean in close to the speaker each night and listen to his favorite radio shows, such as "I Love a Mystery" and "The Green Hornet." He made new friends, most of them other ten-year-olds on a fast track to medical school. There were a few slower boys who would become indifferent salesmen. Jacob played games in an empty lot next to the drugstore. Each day, two enormous cops, both named Tony, cruised by and stopped to give him pats on the head. As a result, Jacob considered the FBI as a future career. His mother took him to Broadway shows, his father to national monuments. Standing in the Botanical Gardens with that short dapper man, Jacob felt protected against the world. Then, in what might have been an omen, he was asked at school to do a painting of a jolly Mexican in a village square. With little talent, he did a creditable job, using bright colors, getting the sombrero just right. Then he introduced brown. Instantly he saw it was a mistake and tried to erase it, smearing the canvas. Then Plotkin showed up and smeared his life.

Each day, after school, Jacob took a glum walk to the drugstore. If Plotkin wasn't there, Jacob would casually ask if anyone had seen him. Inevitably he would be told that Plotkin had "beaten the shit" out of a boy in the playground or in a distant neighborhood. It was almost a relief when Plotkin showed up. At least Jacob wouldn't have to hear of his exploits. Screwing up his courage, he would walk past Plotkin and say, "Hi, Herbie." Plotkin would respond with a nod, then look off in the distance as if he had important matters on his mind. And Jacob would feel released from some brutal obligation – until the following day and the next miserable walk to the drugstore.

There had always been other options. Jacob could have walked to the Concourse and played with a rich boy who had a house full of games. He could have gotten involved in a science project and stayed late at school. Or taken a crosstown bus to discuss sex with a cousin. But he chose to make a daily appearance at the drugstore and to be sick with fear.

And he had never seen Plotkin fight. He had watched him do acrobatic stunts on a bar, twirling his chiseled body high above the playground concrete, and then prepare to fight a bewildered boy who had wandered by. Plotkin had rolled up his sleeves, then delicately removed his wristwatch and placed it on a bench. Jacob could not recall what had happened next. Possibly nothing. But he remembered Plotkin's knuckles, the golden hair on his wrists, the awful ceremony.

One day a boy cried out in the drugstore: "Herbie's fighting a man." Jacob joined a circle that had formed around Plotkin and a wounded veteran of Anzio. The two rolled around in the gutter. But here again, all Jacob saw were muffled blows in the dust and the flash of a metallic leg brace glinting in the sun. When the two were pulled apart, Jacob heard the veteran say: "I would have killed him, but he was a kid." But was he? Jacob and his friends were skinny boys who hadn't grown into their bodies. Jacob himself was given thyroid shots and forced to stand in the malted milk line at summer camp. Plotkin had a powerfully developed body with golden hair in his armpits. Was he a secret man?

As further evidence of his maturity, Plotkin began to show up with a small girl who lived in a cellar. Each day, Jacob watched them cross the vacant lot, Plotkin's arm gallantly draped across her shoulders. Then they ducked down and disappeared into the cellar. Jacob wondered what they did down there. Was Plotkin rough or gentle?

Never once did Plotkin lay a hand on Jacob, which somehow added to his misery. There were times when Jacob wanted to get it over with, to be smashed in the face – so that he could get on with his life. An older boy stopped Jacob one day and said: "I notice Herbie never picks on you." Jacob nodded as if to say "He knows better" – but inwardly he trembled . . .

Jacob had a friend named Nathan, a poor boy whose father sent him out at fourteen to sell endowment policies. He had pitch black hair and broad shoulders. Shy girls who passed him on the street said "Hi, Nate." He was self-assured, but modest in nature and he was a hero to Jacob. One day Jacob and his friend walked past the drugstore. Plotkin was at his post. When he saw Nathan, he looked away.

"You know Herbie?" asked Jacob.

"Yes," said Nathan, "and he knows he's in trouble with me."

Jacob was startled. It was the most amazing thing he had ever heard. Plotkin in trouble with another person? You were supposed to be in trouble with Plotkin. Suddenly he saw the world from a different angle.

Emboldened by the incident, Jacob walked up to Plotkin the following day and slapped him with an open hand, then drew back.

"Let's go, Herbie," he said and put up his hands as if to fight.

A sleepy group looked on, including one adult. This gave Jacob courage. If matters got out of hand, surely they'd intervene. Plotkin slapped Jacob back with equal force, then withdrew, mumbling to himself as if to contemplate the awful consequences if he went further. Jacob virtually flew through the streets in triumph. He'd challenged Plotkin and come away unharmed. But the feeling didn't last. He'd accomplished nothing. Plotkin was still there. He would always be there, until Jacob grew up and moved away. Worse, what if they'd met in an empty lot or in the railroad yard, with no one to intervene. What if Plotkin had ceremoniously taken off his wristwatch and beaten Jacob like a ragdoll. Jacob could feel the golden blows. He pictured his mother tracking down Plotkin's parents and showing them her broken boy.

"Look what you've done to my son," she would say.

The torture continued for Jacob. He couldn't enjoy himself at school, at summer camp, or even watching musical comedies – Plotkin would always be waiting at the drugstore. Waiting for *him*, or so it seemed. There was only one peaceful interlude. A refugee boy ran through the streets one day saying, "Plotkin's got a hernia." Jacob didn't know what a hernia was, only that it had something to do with the groin. He knew that Plotkin would be unable to swing on bars. And that he couldn't fight until it healed. Maybe this would be a good time to get him, to punch him in the hernia, though it wouldn't be fair.

Jacob couldn't wait to see Plotkin and his hernia. The refugee boy said Plotkin's parents had given him a little white dog as a gift, to make up for the operation. On a sunny afternoon, Plotkin made an appearance, walking slowly down the street with the cellar girl, trailed by the little white dog. His gait was awkward, as if he had just ridden an unruly horse. He and the girl entered the cellar, followed by the dog. Jacob imagined that Plotkin had a snow white bandage between his legs, with fringes of golden hair showing. Jacob frankly wanted to look inside the bandage and see what was going on. Maybe the girl would do that in the cellar, remove the bandage and minister to Plotkin's hernia.

The refugee boy told Jacob it took a month for a hernia to heal. For thirty days, Jacob felt carefree and had no need to return to the drugstore. He took advantage of the peaceful interlude by exploring the outer reaches of the Bronx, with particular attention to bridges, construction sites and railroad yards. He interviewed a radio personality for his school newspaper and was amazed at how relaxed and humble the man was, despite his fame. On the cold bathroom tile, Jacob twisted himself into a pretzel and discovered his body. Then Plotkin recovered. As if in celebration, he confronted Jacob on the street and tore a jacket from his body, then danced away. It was blue suede, a birthday gift from Jacob's mother. At a safe distance, Plotkin modeled the jacket, twisting this way and that, posing before an invisible mirror. Jacob knew he could never catch the fleet Plotkin. But he walked toward him, prepared to die. Possibly Plotkin sensed this. Jacob would never know. Tired of the game, Plotkin handed back the jacket. Jacob slipped into it and returned to what he thought of as an unfair life.

Years later, Jacob would learn of Chekhov's dictum: if a gun is introduced in the first act, it must go off by the third. The Plotkin gun in Jacob's life went off, but in other directions. In the school cafeteria, a baby-faced boy punched Jacob in the face. Days later, he was injured in a game of "Rocks." It called for a boy to stand alone in a circle. Rocks were thrown at him, his only protection the lid of a garbage can. When it was Jacob's turn, he covered his face and forgot his knee. He was carried unconscious to Morrisania Hospital. Years later, the Bronx would be remembered as an idyllic place, where everyone lived together in harmony. In truth, it was dangerous; even Jacob's father had a scar on his lip, the result of a subway fight with a shoe salesman.

Slowly, Jacob became less obsessed with Plotkin. He transferred to a distant high school. By the time he got back from his classes each day, the drugstore was closed. At the school newspaper, he was chosen to write a gossip column. He took a busty girl he'd met at summer camp to a production of "Arsenic and Old Lace." Unaware that he was nearsighted, he played some senior basketball. Wearing the handsome team jacket, flushed with academic success, he paraded past the drugstore on a Saturday and saw Plotkin. There were no other boys there. Plotkin stood alone, like a rejected lover.

"How's school, Herbie?" asked Jacob, knowing that Plotkin at best was enrolled at a vocational institute. Plotkin had no answer. His eyes were barren as he looked away. Instantly Jacob was sickened by his own meanness. Then Jacob went off to college in the Far West. The next time he visited the drugstore, he was in Air Force blue – though he was a supply officer and didn't fly. He asked about Plotkin and was told he'd moved away.

Jacob thought he saw Plotkin on the subway, wearing white socks with black shoes, a *Daily News* rolled up in his overcoat. Just what I always expected, Jacob thought, he's got some shitty job in a stockroom. And now he hated himself for his smugness. He took a closer look at the man. It wasn't even Plotkin.

Jacob became a professor of history and philosophy at a community college. He gave a lecture on causation one night, which drew a surprisingly hefty crowd of almost a hundred. Lacking confidence as a speaker, he took a blood pressure pill and was on his game. After the question and answer period, two men approached. He recognized them as being from his old neighborhood. They were a few years younger than Jacob. One had become a dentist, the other a nurse. They talked about the old days.

"What ever happened to Plotkin?" Jacob asked, shaking his head in almost wistful approval. "He was something."

"*He* was something," said the nurse in disbelief.

"What about you?" asked the dentist.

"Me?" said Jacob, touching a hand to his chest. "What are you suggesting?"

The two men looked at Jacob with wounded eyes.

He was stung by their silent accusation. Were they suggesting that he was as bad as Plotkin? How was that possible? Before he could gather himself to respond, he was tapped on the shoulder by a woman who had been in the audience and demanded his attention. The two men disappeared.

Later, as he took the subway to his apartment in Queens, Jacob thought about his encounter with the two men and what they had implied. It's true he'd once had a habit of lowering his head and ramming it into the stomach of his sister's girlfriend. And on occasion, he would jump on the back of a timid schoolmate and ride the unwilling child around the neighborhood as if he were a horse. Perhaps more seriously, he had punched a landlord's son for the crime of being rich and having a room full of expensive toys. For quite some time he'd practiced a wrestler's trick of wrapping his arms around a schoolmate, digging his chin into the boy's chest and forcing him backward to the ground. Come to think of it, he'd once discovered a secret in his chemistry set – by combining two chemicals and jamming them into a gelatin capsule, he could produce a small bomb. He'd tossed such missiles from a rooftop and terrified groups of housewives. Once, he'd emptied the balcony of a theatre by exploding one of his bombs during a Warner Brothers movie. He would have continued creating havoc if he hadn't burned off his eyebrows while mixing up the deadly brew.

As a junior counselor at summer camp, he had awakened small boys at midnight and told them their parents had been executed by Nazis. But to compare these youthful and prankish transgressions to those of Plotkin who had terrorized him for seven long years. This was not only ridiculous, it was a blood libel.

The Convert

"THE JEWS KILLED CHRIST."

Bobby Marcus had seen the hateful declaration scribbled on the walls of tenement buildings in the Bronx, but never before had he heard it spoken aloud. The accusation had been flung at him from the cherry-red lips of a neighborhood Catholic boy, Timmy Flanagan, also seven. Fleet as the wind, Timmy, who rarely walked, only ran, shot down the street, his head thrown back, howling all the way. Bobby did not understand the precise nature of the charge, nor was he prepared to take personal responsibility for the ancient libel. But he knew he was a Jew. Slower than Timmy, he caught up with him later in the day at the corner candy store, standing still for a change and testing chocolates; one with a white center entitled the purchaser to a prize. Bobby easily pinned his adversary to the ground. But Timmy, sensing that Bobby had no violence in him, only shook his head from side to side, convulsed with laughter.

"Don't ever say that again," said Bobby, getting to his feet as if he had accomplished his goal, which was far from clear.

"We'll see about that," said Timmy, as he calmly fluffed up his hair and returned to the counter to fish for prize-winners.

In a vacant lot, months later, the two scuffled once again, their inconclusive struggle broken up by a passing salesman. And in the years that followed, the boys circled each other warily, at a discreet distance, as if probing for a soft spot in the enemy lines. Working as a waiter one summer, Bobby filled out his slender frame and returned from the Jersey shore, anxious to display, if not actually flaunt his newly muscled body in the neighborhood. He headed immediately for the playground; alarmingly, there stood Timmy, calmly dribbling a basketball, towering over every boy in sight, including Bobby.

And thus they traded physical advantage, Bobby nosing ahead several summers later, Timmy drawing even the next – until both went off to college, Bobby to nearby Hofstra, Timmy, with the aid of a divorced father, to far-off Claremont Men's. Then came the Korean War for both young men. Returning home on a brief leave, Bobby proudly strolled the neighborhood streets as an Air Force lieutenant. Coming toward him suddenly was Timmy, a Navy ensign. Both men were flustered and lowered their eyes. Then, if such a thing were possible, they glared at each other shyly. Suddenly, with no words being spoken, they fell into each other's arms in a communion of tears and an undeclared promise of everlasting friendship.

They spent the afternoon together, speaking of failed romance and future glory.

"I never meant that remark I directed at you," said Timmy at one point. "It was just something I heard around the house."

"I gathered that," said Bobby, who hadn't.

No sooner had the friendship been established than Timmy, after his discharge, moved to the West coast, where he studied medicine at Stanford. He became wealthy, not in private practice but as owner and administrator of a thriving group of emergency clinics. Along the way, he married a prominent Jewish oncologist. As a testament to his love for Rebecca Glassman (and as a condition of the marriage) Timmy had completed an arduous eighteen-month conversion to Judaism. (Both bride and groom had retained their names – Glassman and Flanagan.)

Bobby, in the meanwhile, had remained close to home. A high school teacher of Social Studies, he had married a woman who taught the same subject, barely noticing that she was Catholic. He loved her virtually on sight. That was enough. As for his own connection to the Jews, he had never, since his bar mitzvah, set foot in a Synagogue. When pressed to the wall, he would describe himself, obnoxiously, as a "bagel and lox Jew." Slightly aware that he was being a renegade, he took occasional positions that were contrary to the best interests of Israel. On a brief trip to Jerusalem, he and his guide, also secular, posed wearing t'filn at the Western Wall, but only, to the best of his knowledge, as a lark.

The two friends called one another from time to time – and always, sentimentally, on New Year's Eve. They concentrated on major developments, Bobby's knee operation, the birth of Timmy and Rebecca's son. Thus the friendship, slender but unwavering, was kept alive.

The years flashed by – and then one day, Kate and Bobby received a handsomely engraved invitation to the bar mitzvah of Samuel Benjamin Flanagan, son of Timothy Aloysius Flanagan and Rebecca Sylvia Glassman. Timmy enclosed a handwritten note saying that a hotel room had been reserved in Bobby's name.

"I'll be keeping my fingers crossed that you can see your way clear to make it."

Since no mention was made of airline tickets, Bobby assumed he would be expected to pay for them – his friend no doubt taking it for granted that Bobby had prospered over the years – just as Timmy had with the Flanagan Clinics. This was not the case. Despite their combined Board of Education salaries, Bobby and Kate barely kept their heads above water in financially punishing Manhattan.

Bobby and Kate discussed the dent a trip would make in their frail bank account.

"Still and all," said Bobby, "I'd like to go."

"Then it's case closed," said Kate, who had no history of denying Bobby the smallest pleasure. (Bobby, it should be noted, did what he could to hold up his end.)

"And besides," she added, "I've never been to a bar mitzvah."

When Timmy and his wife came out to meet Bobby and Kate at the Sacramento Airport, Bobby was struck by the dramatic change in his friend's appearance. He had expected him to have aged, of course; but Timmy's shoulders were now stooped, he had on rimless glasses, and he had a full head of gray curls, worn much in the style of the noted attorney Alan Dershowitz. To Bobby's way of thinking, Timmy, whose face had once resembled the much remarked upon Map of Ireland, now looked Jewish. Rebecca was a petite, dark-haired woman whose features indicated that she had once been a beauty. But her face now seemed sallow and disappointed. Bobby chalked this up to the strains of preparing for a major religious event. Or perhaps it was the nature and rigors of her medical specialty. Both men took turns introducing their wives, Timmy and Kate exchanging a complex look, an ex-Catholic meeting a casual if not a lapsed one.

As they prepared to leave the terminal, Timmy dropped all formality and embraced Bobby with undisguised emotion.

"To come all the way out here for my kid's bar mitzvah is above and beyond. You have no idea how much this means to me and Becky."

Though he was still unsettled by the steep price of the round-trip tickets, Bobby replied: "I wouldn't have missed it for the world."

A small dinner was held for friends and immediate family that night at Timmy and Rebecca's home, several miles from the city. Timmy mixed cocktails for Bobby and Kate. He said they had bought the spacious Colonial from a Vegas entertainer whose career was on the downslide.

"Frankly, when we first took a look at the place, it was tacky as all get-out. But then Becky here took over," he said, with a fond gesture in his wife's direction, "and voila."

"I did use a decorator," put in the oncologist, modestly.

"Never mind," said Timmy sharply. Then he turned to the visitors. "Trust me . . . it was her eye all the way."

The interior was indeed warm in feeling and tastefully decorated. There were several Chagalls on the walls, originals, for all Bobby knew, and handsome items of Judaica on the various tables and mantelpieces.

Timmy caught Bobby staring at an exquisitely carved Menorah.

"In case you're wondering," said the host, "we picked that baby up in the port of Haifa."

Bobby was seated between Timmy's in-laws. Benjamin Glassman, a retired CPA, barely spoke. When he asked for the salt, it was in a whisper. Mrs. Glassman, a formidable, full-bosomed woman, had the same aggrieved look as her daughter. She brightened only when she learned that Bobby was to be her seatmate. Bobby, no doubt with some presumption, felt he could read her thoughts: "How come my daughter couldn't have met a nice Jewish boy like you?"

After the Hispanic couple – hired for the evening – had served dessert and coffee, Timmy took Bobby aside and asked him what his name was in Hebrew.

Bobby, who could not recall what he had done three nights before, surprised himself by replying instantly.

"Yitzchak."

"Great," said Timmy, scribbling down the name . . . and not even asking how it was spelled.

He then said that Bobby, as a dear friend, would have the honor of reading a section of the torah at the bar mitzvah ceremony. He handed Bobby a sheet of paper with the passage printed in Hebrew; after a quick glance, Bobby was surprised once again. Though it had been years since he had looked at a passage of Hebrew text, he remembered how to pronounce the words, though not their meaning. Then Timmy handed him a tape cassette.

"Listen to this," he said. "It will instruct you on how to chant your passage."

Bobby recalled his own bar mitzvah and his disastrous rendition of the Haftarah. Influenced by the popular baritones of the day – Sinatra, Perry Como, Vic Damone – he had been accused by the Rabbi of "crooning" the section assigned to him; as a punishment, the Rabbi rapped his knuckles in front of the congregation.

"I don't know about the chanting," said Bobby.

"It's important," said Timmy, with a nervous glance at his

mother-in-law. "Just play it a few times. And bear with me on this. It'll be a piece of cake."

In the hotel room that night, Bobby was increasingly upset by the chanting requirement. He had, quite frankly, seen the trip as something of a pleasurable vacation – and he was in no mood to embark upon what amounted to a program of study, however brief.

"Where am I supposed to get a player?" he asked Kate, flipping the cassette up and down as if preparing to throw it at someone.

"I'll call down to room service," said Kate. "I'm sure they have one."

"Don't bother," said Bobby. "I'll read – but I'm not chanting. First of all, I'm jet-lagged. Second of all, it's a performance, no matter how you slice it. I don't like to do things half-assed. . . . It would take a week to get it right. He should have told me about this before we got here."

"And besides," he said, tossing the cassette aside. "I notice he didn't pay for the hotel room either."

The ceremony was held in a light and airy synagogue that did not differ much in design from a church Bobby had admired while attending the christening of Kate's nephew in upstate New York. A basket, overbrimming with yarmulkes, had been set aside for visitors in the reception area. Bobby chose one that was snow white, and also a taleth, although the selection was much more limited.

Kate watched him solemnly drape the prayer shawl around his shoulders, as if he were warming himself in a forest.

"Are you supposed to do that?" she asked.

"Of course," said Bobby, taking her hand and leading her into the synagogue proper.

As the Congregationalists filed into the house of worship, the Rabbi, a neatly-dressed woman with a short no-nonsense hairdo, set the tone for the ceremony by chanting a wordless melody. Her voice was high and clear and quite lovely, calling up visions of a warriors' campfire on the eve of battle in ancient Judea. Still, the guests seemed to ignore her as they greeted one another, exchanging reports of recent vacations, primarily in Palm Springs. Bobby thought this was rude of them and said as much to the neatly dressed man who sat beside him. He seemed frail, as if recovering from an illness.

"Where I come from they show respect," said Bobby.

"It's just till they settle down," the man assured Bobby. "And where are you from?"

"New York."

"Really? I was from there, too."

True to the man's word, when the Rabbi began to speak, the congregation fell silent.

She welcomed the group to the special occasion, expressing gratitude to those who had traveled great distances to attend young Samuel's bar mitzvah. In the front row, Timmy, also wearing a yarmulke and beautifully embroidered taleth, had been bent over, as if in advance prayer. At the mention of "visitors from afar," he turned and gave Bobby a thumbs up.

The ceremony began. Bobby soon learned, with some mild disappointment, that he was not the only honoree. At least a dozen friends and relatives of the Glassmans – most in the medical profession – had also been asked to read Torah selections. Bobby was next to last on the list and had to wait with discomfort as each of the honorees chanted their Torah passages flawlessly. He consoled himself by deciding they were experienced Congregationalists. Or they had put in long hours of preparation.

When Bobby's turn came, he mounted the platform and saw his selection spread out before him in large print. But unlike the version that had been given to him by Timmy, these Hebrew letters had no vowel markings, making it impossible for him to read the words correctly. Not only did he fail to chant, but as he stumbled through the selection, he mispronounced at least a dozen words in the brief passage, each blunder drawing a sharp look from the Rabbi.

His ears were hot as he took a seat beside Kate.

"You were terrific," she said, squeezing his arm supportively.

"The hell I was."

The ceremony continued, a high point being the recitation of a long Torah passage by the bar mitzvah boy, whose delivery was youthfully impeccable. Samuel was a cheerful-looking redhead, who appeared to have picked up the best features of his parents – Timmy's nose, his mother's great eyes – and then added a puckish third dimension of his own. Timmy and Rebecca looked on with pride as their son delivered a speech in English about the importance of protecting the environment on behalf of generations to come – and not just his own.

The Rabbi then gathered Samuel, his parents, and the Glassmans around her, thanking Timmy and Rebecca for providing their son with a wonderful Jewish upbringing. As the Rabbi blessed the little group, Timmy looked at Mrs. Glassman, as if for approval; his mother-in-law's response was to crane her head in another direction. Once again, Bobby felt he could read her thoughts: "He can convert all he wants. And I don't care if he's a doctor or a lawyer or even a dentist. I'm not buying the package."

To conclude the ceremony, a processional, led by Timmy and Samuel, each holding a Torah, walked solemnly through the synagogue, a number of Congregationalists leaning out of the aisle to touch their prayer shawls to the sacred scrolls, then to kiss the fringes. Bobby remembered seeing the ritual as a boy; he had always wanted to try it, which he did.

"It was a beautiful ceremony," said Kate, as they left the house of worship and walked into blinding sunlight.

"I agree," said Bobby. "And I wish Timmy luck with those in-laws."

Bobby and Kate stayed on that night for a celebratory buffet dinner and dance at Timmy's country club. Several hundred people were on hand for the affair. To spice up the proceedings, a master of ceremonies and disc jockey had been hired. He alternated recordings of hip-hop selections favored by Samuel and his friends with standards for the older group. Also mixed in were tunes from Broadway shows with Jewish themes such as "Milk and Honey" and "Fiddler on the Roof." Though Kate was more of a Stones person, she and Bobby danced dreamily to several Sinatra ballads. Bobby's legs were in good shape for the spirited Horah that followed, enabling him to execute the tricky cross-kicks with ease and precision. When "four strong men" were called for to hoist first Timmy, then Samuel and finally Rebecca aloft in chairs – and to dance them about – Bobby was the first to volunteer.

Throughout much of the festivities, Bobby had little contact with his friend. He watched Timmy circulate among the guests, smoking a cigar, accepting gift envelopes, which he deposited in his breast pocket with a little pat for each one, as if to say, "Never fear, I'll take good care of this." Bobby made a mental note to send his own gift check to Samuel – as soon as he got home – another expense he'd forgotten about. It was only late in the evening that Timmy, his bowtie loosened at the collar, made his way to the buffet table where Bobby had returned for a second helping.

"Got enough food?" asked Timmy.

"Plenty," said Bobby, scooping up a spoonful of noodle pudding, an old favorite. "It's a great party."

"I'm glad you're enjoying it. But frankly, I was a little disappointed that you didn't chant your selection."

"I'm sorry about that, Timmy. There wasn't time to get it right. I thought I'd just say the words."

"You didn't do such a hot job at that either."

"I don't know if you're aware of it," said Bobby, putting aside his plate and trying to suppress his annoyance, "but on the version they gave me, there weren't any vowels."

"Then answer me this: How come everybody else chanted without vowels?"

"I can't speak for them. The bottom line is, I wasn't in the mood."

"Your mood's got nothing to do with it," said Timmy, pointing a finger at Bobby. "It wouldn't have killed you to chant. I spent a fortune on this affair, and you brought down the whole occasion."

"Now you're exaggerating."

"Bullshit," said Timmy. "The Rabbi was pissed and Becky wasn't too happy about it either. I don't even want to discuss my in-laws. Added to which I saw that move you made when the kid and I carried out the Torahs."

"What are you talking about?"

"Touching the tsitsis to one of them, to make up for not chanting."

"That's not why I did it."

"The hell it wasn't."

"Now look . . ."

"No, *you* look."

And suddenly, to the background strains of "If I were a Rich Man," they were at each other and went tumbling head over heels in a furious Judaic pinwheel of gefilte fish, kasha varnischkes, chopped liver canapés and derma with gravy.

Bobby pressed his thumbs on the convert's throat, debating whether to choke him or take out his eyes.

"We did kill Christ, you Jew bastard," he cried out, "and you better get used to it."

The Investigative
Reporter

ALEXANDER KAHN, a failed novelist, and at best a marginal producer of off-Broadway plays, decided at age forty-five to go back to his beginnings and try to get the knot of his life untangled. Trained as a journalist, he got a job as a reporter for a small Long Island daily and for several months wrote competent stories about local politics. When his marriage broke up, he had held on, perhaps idiotically, to his ten-room house in the suburbs. To be close to his job, he moved back into it. He had lived alone in an empty apartment. Why not an empty house?

One day, he was surprised to learn that his managing editor, a prison reform man, had gotten him a chance to cover a small correctional unit in the South, one that was proud of its facilities and its record on rehabilitation. Kahn had never been inside a prison and had always wondered about them. How long could he last in one? Would he be able to stand up to the homosexual advances? Could he exist on prison food? Would he soon begin to bang his head on the walls? What if he didn't like his cellmate? (When he asked himself that question, he used the word 'roommate'.) He was excited about the assignment, although he was a little nervous about it as well. Though he had traveled widely in Europe, he had never been to the South and thought of it as a hostile place where people would look at him through narrowed eyes. In the Air Force, a Southerner had once said he was soft in the crotch. Kahn, a powerful man, although misleadingly frail in appearance, had started for the fellow, then veered off. The words had barely been audible. Perhaps he had heard them wrong. Still,

31

he was confident that in the South, one way or another, he would get his head broken.

After a three-hour flight, Kahn rented a car to take him to the prison. As he stepped off the plane, he could have sworn he smelled barbecue sauce. But as he drove the seventy miles to the prison, there didn't seem to be much South in evidence. Perhaps an occasional indication of it – a Fox Run, a Buzzard Emporium – but for the most part, with its myriad service stations and fast food spots, it reminded him of the discarded outer peelings of any large city in the North. He stopped once to eat local red snapper in a luncheonette. Leaning across the counter to reach for extra French fries, he saw shotguns stacked near the soup bowls. As he ate his fish, a fellow in the next booth, for no apparent reason, began to kick hard at his table legs, as if to chop them down. Maybe this was Southern stuff, he thought.

Kahn had never been to a prison and wasn't quite sure how you got at one. Did you just walk up to it and knock on the door? From the outside, the prison seemed drab and generalized, an electronics firm that kept missing out on lush defense contracts. He found the Warden's office easily enough. Just outside was an exhibition entitled: "A So-Called 'Harmless' Utensil." A rack of malevolent-looking weapons, worse than knives, had been arrayed in a glass cabinet; each had been fashioned out of a toothbrush. A Chicano guard approached and said: "They make some beautiful stuff, don't they." His eyes were moist and wondrous, as if he was looking at a famous statue. Kahn had never spoken to a Chicano before and was surprised – shamefully – to find him in a guard's uniform, not on the inside. The guard took him to see the Warden, a stocky man who wore a neat wedding band and had a fat and friendly neck of the kind that got pinched by granddaughters. The guard took a seat in the Warden's office, as if he, too, were going to be in on the proceedings, but the Warden made a disapproving face and the guard slipped into the corridor.

"What can I do for you, Mr. Kahn?" asked the Warden.

Kahn reminded him that he was the one who'd been sum-
moned to the prison. The Warden scratched his head and said,
"Oh yes, I forgot." Kahn enjoyed the man's absent-mindedness,
although it seemed an unusual quality for a Warden. Did he forget where he put prisoners, too? The Warden said he had come
up through the ranks, starting his career as a 'picket'. Kahn enjoyed hearing the word, his first taste of prison slang. The Warden
said he lived on the prison grounds with a houseboy who was an
ax murderer but behaved gently so long as he was inside the
prison.

"Outside, though, Wheeler can't cope."

Kahn did not like the idea of anyone having a houseboy in this
day and age, but he let it pass, reminding himself that he didn't
come down there for a debate.

The Warden had a new intercom and ordered two coffees; he
seemed more interested in trying out the equipment than in the
beverage. A secretary brought in two hot cups of it; her face was
gray and concerned, as if she was in a constant state of emergency. There was a racket behind a door in the Warden's office.
The official opened it brusquely, his first show of impatience.
Kahn caught a glimpse of men in Stetsons who looked like board
members and others who might have been prisoners, all boiling
up together in an adjoining room. The Warden looked in, mut-
tered something and slammed the door, taking care not to let
Kahn look inside at what may have been all his prison troubles, in
the one room. As the Warden sat down, Kahn noticed that it was
hard to get a clean look at him; one side of his face seemed to be
glassed-off, a prison in itself. Kahn concluded that he had an injury, from an old rebellion. He noticed, too, that the Warden was-
n't quite so stocky after all; the effect came from a bullet-proof
vest.

"Did I arrive at a bad time?" asked Kahn.

"We're having trouble at our hard-core Unit . . . Pardee."

Of course they were having trouble at their hard-core unit,
Kahn thought. That's what hard-core meant, didn't it. But Kahn

liked the Warden's frankness. On his own, there was little chance Kahn would have found out about the recalcitrant unit.

"I guess you have to be on your toes every second in a job like this."

The Warden snickered. He didn't spend any time being ingratiating, which Kahn appreciated. He led Kahn to a "transfer station" where prisoners were held temporarily before being shifted to other units. To take one step, you had to wait until a gate slammed shut behind you. Then another one opened. Kahn couldn't imagine the actual prison being any more secure than the transfer facility.

"I guess that's when they're the most dangerous," he said. "When they're being shoved around."

"Something like that," said the Warden.

From his wallet, he took an old folded-up picture of prisoners in a van with iron collars around their necks, one collar linked to the next. "That's how they used to get moved," he said, "in Black Nellies."

He shook his head in vague amusement at the good old days, then put the picture back in his wallet. It took them awhile to weave their way through the steel puzzle. When the last gate shut behind them, they broke free into the Prison Yard, an immaculately appointed space the size of a football field. In the center stood a dazzling modernistic sculpture, a mythical creature stretching its wings to the sky, hooves struggling in tropical shrubbery, all of it exploding with concrete beauty. Kahn thought he recognized the work as that of Barnet Mandel, a sculptor who had been jailed in his lifetime for his support of extreme left-wing causes. Was Mandel showing his solidarity with the prisoners? Or perhaps with the prison, for being so forward-looking? Either way, it was amazing that Southern board members had allowed it to be there. A hundred or so prisoners stood about in shy clusters of three and four, trying not to look at Kahn and the Warden. They wore almost surgically white uniforms and might have been hospital employees. Kahn was unprepared for such cleanliness. He had assumed that a prison would have a kind of prison smell, in the way of all public facilities, but this one didn't.

"Do they wear the same uniforms at Pardee?" he asked.

"The exact same," said the Warden.

In one section of the Yard black inmate wrestlers, naked to the waist, pawed at each other in the dirt like lion cubs. The Warden said they were members of a crack wrestling team that would compete in another part of the state, all proceeds going to recreational facilities for the prison. They had an inordinate number of scars on them – still, Kahn marveled at the shape they were in, also the terrific physical condition of the other inmates. He was in decent shape himself, but for all his efforts, still a little slack around the middle. He saw a few teams of older fellows in great black-socketed sunglasses go limping by on crutches.

"What about them?" he asked.

The sun tipped against the glassed-off section of the Warden's face. He said something about threshing machines, but his voice was barely audible.

"It's funny," said Kahn, after inhaling in vain to try to pick up some kind of prison smell, "you can imagine what a prison yard would look like, but you can't actually get the feel of it till you're in one."

The Warden said nothing. Kahn decided to make no further comments along that line.

Discreetly salted among the prisoners were almost absurdly young guards. They carried no guns, giving their empty holsters an open-snouted look, like fish gasping for air. The Warden led Kahn up a street ramp to the Prison dining room. It was empty, but the tables were neatly set and covered with cloths so blindingly white that Kahn almost felt he had to turn his head away. There were four place settings to a table, arranged in geometrical precision.

"They're not allowed to talk when they eat," said the Warden, amazingly answering a question Kahn was going to ask. "It works out better that way."

Kahn, who loved fresh vegetables – and had recently taken to steaming them to seal in the flavor – suddenly smelled wonderful ones, hot and spicy and aromatic. The Warden led him over to the serving counter where proud prison chefs in great white hats stood beaming over vats of them – not only string beans and carrots, but also more obscure varieties that Kahn rarely got to eat such as okra and turnips, all simmering in their own hot juices. In truth, the meat didn't look that terrific, but the overall aroma was profound and seductive; Kahn felt it was his first real contact with the South since he'd arrived.

"The vegetables sure do look appetizing," he said, longing for a heaping plate of them, but too shy to ask.

"An inmate can have any five he likes," said the Warden. (So why not just two for me, thought Kahn.)

"We grow our own," the Warden continued. "That's why they're so fresh. Of course, you'd get tired of it after four or five years, like anything else, and yearn for a pizza."

Again, Kahn was struck by the Warden's balanced attitude – but he was still disappointed when he wasn't asked to sit down and have a plateful of the vegetables.

"Would you like to go into the cellblock?" he asked Kahn.

"Of course," said the visitor, who wasn't quite sure what the invitation entailed. Once, in the service, a Major had asked Kahn if he would like to shoot landings in a night-fighter. He'd said yes, and before he knew it, he was vomiting acrobatically in the sky. Kahn started to walk toward a white building with bars on the window.

"No, no," said the Warden, "that's the hospital. You don't want them sawing your nuts off."

It was the Warden's first tasteless remark; still, Kahn decided to write it off as rough-hewn correctional humor. The Warden led Kahn to yet another building, this one older than the hospital. For a moment, it reminded Kahn of the apartment house in which he had grown up, before his father made a little money in shoulder pads. It also occurred to him that perhaps most of the prison funds were put into outward display – the sculpture in the Yard, the spotless dining room – and that the cellblock itself would be a hellhole. But it wasn't quite true. The cellblock appeared to be a decent place, on the order of an old public school. He wasn't quite prepared for all the steel, also the small amount of space between the bars. Only exceptionally slim fellows would be able to stick their arms through. Again, the building had a pleasant smell to it, which was surprising, considering all the tense bodies that were packed together in there. The Warden said that all the prisons were built as maximum security units. If they got a nicer group of inmates, they could always thin out the security. But the opposite wasn't true. "You can lighten up, but you can't tighten up," said the Warden, using what Kahn assumed was a slogan for board meetings.

"Am I seeing a typical facility?" asked Kahn.

"Pretty much," said the Warden. "Although I guess Pardee is a little tougher."

Maybe I should be over at Pardee after all, Kahn thought. On the other hand, the Warden didn't have to bring up the subject of Pardee at all. They walked up three flights of skeletal stairs, everything above and below them visible, the same with the sides. If you scratched your ear, they could spot it from one end of the prison to the other. When they got to the third tier, the Warden stopped and said: "This one's as good as any." A guard opened a gate and Kahn had the sensation of being shoved lightly into a cellblock. Suddenly, he was alone in a small space with seventy odd prisoners. He hadn't expected the Warden to remain outside, but again, it was no doubt in the interest of being fair. If the Warden accompanied him, the prisoners would probably clam up and there would go Kahn's objective view of life behind bars. Some of the inmates were in their cells – they looked almost like doll houses for children – while others watched a Western on television, in the thin strip of space that made up the day room. Kahn felt a light tremor of panic – he had a history of blacking out in confined places – but he settled himself down. The prisoners seemed to be waiting for him to say something.

"Hi," he said, "I'm with a newspaper on Long Island."

At first, he looked through them, his eyes focused on no one in particular, but then he decided to single out one man – his theatre training – and talk directly to him. He probably picked the wrong fellow, a powerful white man with a lot of cut marks and tattoos and syrupy features that appeared ready to slide down his face. So he quickly shifted over to a younger man with a shy smile and rural features, one he took to be an injured ranch hand. Thus anchored, Kahn was able to sweep his eyes around and talk to everyone. Apart from the fellow with the cut marks, they seemed to be a friendly group. He particularly liked a sleepy Mexican with a fat junkie's nose who was listening attentively while his hands pretended to carve something invisible in his lap. Kahn had to remind himself that he wasn't in hard-core Pardee. But maybe Pardee wasn't so bad either. A prisoner, who really didn't seem to care, asked Kahn how to get started in writing; he gave him a tip or two and then said: "I'm trying to get started myself." They laughed at that. The give and take went on, lightly, superficially, Kahn all the while wondering if he could survive in such a place. He decided that if he had to, he could get on nicely, although he was over the norm in the age department. He had been worried about the smell. It smelled just fine. He would avoid the fellow with the cut marks, or perhaps challenge him quickly in the tool-and-die shop and get it over with. He would try to room with the shy ranch hand. If they got the Mexican in with them, they would have an unbeatable trio. Who would dare to fuck with them – three principled but quietly hard men, including Kahn himself, no pushover, especially after he had toughened himself up a bit behind bars. Once he got used to the narrowness of the bars, and all the noise the steel made, he would be fine. The exercise yard was a big plus. He loved volleyball. And oh those vegetables! Imagine getting any five you wanted, every day of the week! How could anyone tire of those delicious little treats, even after years of confinement?

"Make sure you put me in your movies," said a chubby, good-natured black fellow who thought Kahn was a director. Kahn realized he had been in the cellblock for twenty minutes, right in the center of check-forgers and possible ax-murderers. When he had first come in, he had been afraid to touch them for fear of being contaminated or taken hostage. Now he was ready to move in with them. He wished them well. They made him promise to drop by again and bring along some "goody-goods" (for this, they made a dope-smoking sign). He could have sworn that even the cut-up fellow's face softened a bit just before he left. As he walked out of the cellblock he took a quick look at the TV set and was surprised at the clarity of the picture, every bit as good as the one he had in his house on Long Island.

"It wasn't too bad in there," said Kahn, as they circled a pair of handball courts in the prison yard.

"Yeah," said the Warden, allowing himself a trace of bitterness, "and we're supposed to be backward."

Off in the distance, Kahn spotted gray sheds and some tense activity in the dust.

"That's where they keep the dogs," said the Warden.

"Are they trained to kill?"

"No, just to track down an escapee and scare the shit out of him. Of course, we don't get too many."

Well, that was fair enough, Kahn thought. What was the prison supposed to do, let them walk out of there? Child-molesters and killers? Just as long as the dogs didn't tear somebody's leg off.

The Warden led Kahn on a brisk tour of the laundry where the bone white tablecloths and uniforms were turned out; then they visited the "tag" shop, the automotive training unit and a facility that made dentures for the whole state.

"At sixty dollars a set," the Warden said, holding one up and chopping the air with it, "they're the equal of any in the Sun Belt."

Outside the Denture Unit, the Warden excused himself, turning Kahn over to a short and edgy man in his fifties, Father
Campesano, the prison padre. Kahn had the feeling that he had
once been jovial and twinkly-eyed in the traditional manner and
then given up the style. The padre told Kahn that whenever there
was a rebellion, in previous administrations, he was the first to be
taken hostage; several years back, he had been caught, twirling
like a weathervane, in the middle of a shoot-out.

"My stomach's supposed to go this way," he said, lifting his
cassock and pointing, good-naturedly, to a network of scars, "and
instead it goes that way."

As they walked through the Yard, the fidgety padre peered
about, as if to check for snipers. He had an ax to grind with grifters
and con men, who for some reason annoyed him more than mass
murderers.

"I'd put your domestic killer back on the street in a minute,"
he said. "He did it once, that's it. But a con man's got a sheet fifteen
pages long. He was born with one leg and, spoiled devil that he is,
he's never learned to get by on that one leg. A con man will never
mend his ways."

Despite his edginess, the padre still held on to a reservoir of
kindness – or so Kahn felt – and the prisoners were lucky to have a
man like that around.

Prisoner art hung on the walls of the library, clowns and bull-
fighters, blandly sketched. Kahn tried in vain to find one rough
jewel in the batch. The prisoners were all penned up. He was positive that their art, if allowed to flow freely, would be hot and sexual. Maybe a lot of it was, but why should the Administration put
such works on display? Was it the Rhode Island School of Design?
Of course not. It was a prison. Scanning the shelves, Kahn found
only books on tannery work and pig iron. Disappointed, he asked
the padre: "Don't you have any other kinds of books?" The padre,
possibly praying behind a world Atlas, gestured silently toward a
partition. Kahn walked that way, noting with irony that the library
was the one section of the Prison that had the bad smell he was

worried about. On the other side of a divider, and through a door, Kahn came upon a small and charming section, uncannily similar to the library he remembered from his old neighborhood where he went each afternoon to leaf through *The Wonderful Adventures of Nils*, a favorite. Stacked neatly in old-fashioned covers were hardy perennials such as *Dombey and Son* and *Gone with The Wind*. No bestsellers were in evidence, but there were some surprise entries such as *Decline and Fall* and *If It Die*. If you'd asked him, Kahn would have expected to find the kinds of books given to people in hospitals such as *Cycling Through Vancouver*. It occurred to Kahn that if he were doing time in the prison – and it was permitted – he could really "read around" in such a library, and with enormous pleasure. By quick estimate, he guessed there were at least two or three years' worth of treats in there, before he would have to double back. Reflexively, and not without hope, his eyes traveled over to the "K" section. There on the shelf, between Kaffle and Kensington was *The Settlement*, by Alexander Kahn, his own first novel, written eighteen years before, a book that had sold only modestly but had been received nicely by a handful of serious critics. Kahn's second novel, more ambitious, had been annihilated by the very same critics, joined by others. This had given him a sick feeling that never went away. Losing heart, he had become a producer.

"Padre," he shouted to Campesano, who was still praying in the technical section, "my book's on the shelf."

He put his hands over his eyes to cover the embarrassing tears, but then he realized he was with a man of God; it was all right to cry in front of him.

"Let's see," said the padre.

Kahn took down the copy. "This is really something," he said, genuinely fighting for breath, "I didn't even know there were any copies in print. And to find it in a prison."

He opened the book. It was in fairly good condition – far from dog-eared – but it had been taken out and stamped at least thirty times. That meant it had been read by thirty prisoners, not to mention their cellmates who might have taken a peek at it, too. The book was about his father, cheated out of his life's savings by unscrupulous business partners in the shoulder pad business. What could the prisoners have possibly gotten out of such a book? But at least thirty of them now knew the kind of man his father was – decent, honorable, although a little too trusting. This made him cry again.

"Look," he said, turning arbitrarily to a page and pointing to the word 'Negro'. (Mostly he was trying to keep himself from crying.) "I wrote it eighteen years ago, before everybody said 'black'."

"Isn't that something," said the padre. "Let me tell the Warden."

He buzzed the Warden on the intercom. "Hey, Hollis," he said. "Come on down. Our visitor's found a book he wrote on the shelf. I told him, of course, it should be in the porno section."

Kahn understood that the padre was trying to lighten things up, but he didn't care for the joke. He was too moved.

The Warden ran in, out of breath, as if there were a prison emergency. Kahn showed him the book.

"That's wonderful," said the official. "What's it about?"

Kahn told him it was a thinly autobiographical novel that focused on his father's losses in the shoulder pad business. "But it has other dimensions, too," he added.

"I'm delighted we had it here," said the Warden, beaming proudly, as if an ex-inmate had turned up with a responsible job.

"Yeah," said the padre, "and just think, it never even occurred to him that we might have switched it in here just before he showed up."

The Warden and the padre laughed and Kahn joined in with them, although he wasn't too crazy about that joke either.

It was getting late. Kahn replaced the book on the shelf, tenderly, as if he were ending a visit to an inmate. "Maybe I'll get back to writing," he said.

On the steps of the Library, Kahn asked the Warden if there was anything in the prison he had missed.

"We could visit Ureah," said the Warden, "the women's unit."

"What's it like over there?"

"Nicer-looking," said the Warden. "Lots of pastels."

Then, stroking his heavy chin, he said: "Holly Kitenzo's bringing a suit against us for not allowing her to wear her hair extremely short. You could see her."

"What's she in for?"

"Bank robbery," said the Warden. "Also aggravated assault. She left four dead in Arkansas. Here's her petition."

He handed Kahn a sheet of paper with tiny printing on it and diagrams. It looked like the floor plan of a bank for a planned robbery. He may have been shirking his responsibilities, but suddenly Kahn had no heart to visit Ureah. An older man and a friend had once suggested to him that sometimes people had to protect themselves from the world's horrors. Here was his chance to start. The day had been exhausting. Finding the book about his beloved father had been an overwhelming experience. As far as he was concerned, it was enough that the Warden had told him about Kitenzo so that he didn't find out about it on CNN.

"I think I'll pass," said Kahn. "But you know what I would like?"

"What's that?" asked the Warden.

"A plate of your vegetables."

"Why didn't you say so," said the Warden. "I'll have them warmed up."

"It just occurred to me," said Kahn.

"Padre," said the Warden, "get Mr. Kahn a container of our vegetables."

"Coming right up," said the padre.

Kahn hadn't meant to inconvenience the man of God, but before he could protest, the padre had whisked himself off to the dining room. Kahn and the Warden stood in silence on the prison steps. Off in the distance, some petrochemical works were lighting up, giving the prison grounds a bejeweled look.

The padre came out with a container of cooked vegetables and handed them to Kahn.

"I hope they travel well," said the padre.

"About as good as I will," said Kahn, not quite sure what he meant.

"Come back and visit us," said the Warden, shaking Kahn's hand. "Any time."

"I'd like that," said Kahn, feeling an urge to pinch the man's friendly neck.

He said goodbye to the padre, then watched the two prison officials enter the facility. Alone in the night, Kahn took a last look at the prison and sneaked a taste of the hot vegetables; they'd gone heavy on the okra which was every bit as good as he'd imagined. The prison lights blinked on. Kahn caught an outline of two men playing ping-pong. He pictured others in the cellblocks, reading books from the excellent library, writing letters home, playing comradely games of cards and watching TV on the wonderfully clear set he'd spotted in the day room. They were probably exchanging bawdy stories, too. Who knows, possibly a cart had been wheeled through, carrying still more vegetables, ones that were left over from lunch – cold, but still delicious. He thought of his new friends, the padre, the ranch hand, the sleepy Mexican, even the man with the cut-marks who probably wasn't that terrible once you got to know him. More than ever, he was convinced that he could get along very nicely if he was ever thrown into a prison like this.

Then he pictured his gloomy house in the suburbs. Kahn was the only single on the street. Once in awhile, he dropped into a bar nearby that attracted divorcees, most of them too flashy for his taste. Now and then, he watched a movie in an ancient theatre down the street, one of the few customers. Jolson had once played there, but this meant nothing to Kahn. Most nights he worked in his attic, looking out on darkness.

He hated to leave the prison and for a moment considered knocking on the prison door and asking the Warden for another quick tour, in case he had overlooked some details. But that was ridiculous. It was late. He had a deadline. What if he missed his plane! Rummaging around for his car keys, his fingers touched a joint from an old forgotten party. At first he was terrified. After all, he was still on prison grounds. The state was famous for having the toughest laws on dope in the country, and this is where they put the dopers. But then hands other than his own seemed to pull the forbidden joint out of his pocket and light it up. Unmistakably, though, it was Alexander Kahn himself who took a puff and held it flamboyantly aloft in the moonlight. At a nearby guard-post, a dog flared its nostrils, then pricked up its ears. Two others did the same. Kahn watched them start tentatively in his direction, then gather speed and flash swiftly through the night. Guards followed them as the prison lights came up white-hot and a voice on the bullhorn said: "Stay where you are." Scared out of his wits, and at the same time shivering with anticipation, Kahn prepared to embrace his new freedom.

"I Don't Want Her, You Can Have Her . . ."

THE MAN AND WOMAN sat opposite one another in the parlor of a West Village brownstone. The room had a cozy disorganized look to it, as if it had been shared by a devoted and dotty couple for the past thirty or forty years – which it had not. The man, in his fifties and not unattractive, had not shaved for several days. His "look" was not, in this case, a fashion statement. The woman, twenty years his junior, had close-cropped hair and wore a tailored suit.

The man took a deep breath as if he were about to plunge into cold water.

"She's become fat."

"Fat," the woman said cheerfully, repeating the key word, as if to hold it up to the light for inspection. He had some familiarity with this therapeutic technique, although this was the first time it had been directed at him (*used* against him?) personally.

"I don't mean *gross*," he said, retreating a bit. "Although I did catch her doing a fat walk the other day, waddling if you must know, as if she were preparing to go all out and really pork up. And there is something about the way she's begun to guard her food, her pasta dishes, to be precise – leaning forward and encircling the plate with her arms and looking about on all sides as if someone were going to snatch it away. Like fucking Cro Magnon man is the appearance of it. And she'll snap at me if I so much as touch one of her french fries, pretending to be playful, although, trust me, that is far from the case.

47

"Actually," he said, "I'm talking about forty or fifty pounds.

"Sixty max," he added.

He allowed for a pause here – in the event she wanted to move in with a comment. He was not disappointed when she chose to let him go on.

"You have to understand," he said, "she had a beautiful body when we met – lovely full breasts, a small waist, athletic legs – *schoolyard* legs is the way I thought of them. Every boy's dream she was, if you'll permit me."

"I'll permit you," she said, and of course they could have done ten minutes on the word "permit" but they both decided to push on.

"My own daughter," he said, "who was naturally resistant to my remarrying, said she could see why I would want to sleep with her. 'Roll around' with her is the way she put it.

"There was more to it, of course," he continued, not waiting for a response this time. "Her laugh, a chuckle, really . . . eyes at the same time both trusting and mischievous . . . very difficult to pull off. We shared the same taste in books, although lately she's gone off in another direction . . . reads novels about large Irish families. Large *dysfunctional* Irish families . . . I'm sure it's just a phase. . . . Much more important is that in time I began to feel she was the most compassionate person I'd ever known. And good Christ, she felt so good in bed."

"And now?"

"And now," he repeated, throwing the technique right back at her to gain a little time, since the next part was going to be tricky. He had never had a female therapist before and did not want to go at the sex business too hard. Nor was there any point in being overly decorous. Pussy-footing around. (And there was a phrase for you.)

"She still *feels* good. After all, it *is* her, for Christ's sakes. And I do love her."

He began to cry at that point, not a great big blubbering affair, but he was crying all right, although he would have bet a great deal of money against his falling apart in such a manner. Certainly not during a first session.

"Do you want a tissue?" she asked.

"No, no, that's fine," he said, brushing at the tears with his shirt sleeve.

"If I had to describe the sex," he said, regrouping – and accepting the tissue after all, "I'd call it comfortable. Cozy, if you wish.

"And I'm sure you'll agree there's a lot worse," he added, picking up some snappishness in his tone.

"I do agree," she said, taking the traditional – and much celebrated – non-committal stance.

"I can assure you," he continued, though she had not asked for assurance, "I've never humiliated her, never come out and said 'Good God, you're huge or hummed a chorus of 'She's too fat for me.' Gone by the textbook I have, leading by example, keeping my own weight down, or at least attempting to. I may have gotten off a remark here and there about a girlfriend of hers who's remained trim and fit – but nothing *cruel*.

"Still, I must have indicated to her one Sunday night – that's the time we set aside to – as they say – *do* it . . . that the weight bothered me. Perhaps it was the way I put my arms around her waist – a bit dramatically – as if to suggest that it took some effort to get all the way around her. Or it might have been the expression on my face when she undressed – I'm not much of a poker player. In any case, she seemed to get the idea and suggested I flip her around, close my eyes and think of the photo affixed to her college I.D. card – the one I had always found arousing. That was her proposal, and that's what we do, once a week, me focusing on the photo on her college I.D. card, making love . . . and here I suppose I have to use the phrase 'doggie-style.'"

"I won't tell a soul," she said, showing a mischievous side of her own.

"I do love to kiss her. I get lost when I kiss her," he went on, getting lost as he said this. "There isn't anyone else I'd rather kiss."

"Anyone else," she said, and this time the repetition was irritating, taking him, as it did, to a place he didn't particularly want to go.

"There *is* someone else," he said. "A Russian woman of all people. Highly unlikely choice for me, if indeed it *was* a choice on my part. Attractive, slender, of course . . . quite young. She'd read something of mine in translation . . . took me to dinner, made it clear she's available . . . lives alone, writes a little pornography . . . All of this attention from her was flattering . . . and yet I've held back. It seems too exhausting to have an affair. And of course there was one troubling aspect to it."

"Tell me about it."

"After our dinner, my new friend asked if it was customary to leave a tip."

"Well. . . . coming from Russia . . ."

"I realize that . . . different culture . . . It's all very reasonable . . . Except that she pronounced the word 'teep.' Call it xenophobic if you like, but I could never have an affair with someone who says 'teep.' By the time she got it right, I'd be off in another direction.

"Besides," he said, almost as an afterthought, "what if my wife found out? . . . ."

"What if she did?"

"That's my fear, you see. That she would immediately lose fifty pounds and run off with one of those befuddled third World diplomats that she counsels at the UN."

"And then?"

"And then?" he said, brought up short for the moment. "And then I wouldn't *have* her."

She glanced at the clock. He did as well and saw that the session was drawing to a close.

"Look," he said, rushing now to meet the deadline, "I can get through very nicely. It's pleasant enough in bed. I don't claim to have any ferocious drive these days. It's not as if I'm lusting after skinny blondes in garter belts. She's an awfully good friend and tremendously loyal. I know, I know, it sounds like I'm describing a dog. But she's a remarkable person. How many men have that? What I'm getting at is that this is not a sad story."

"What is it that you want?"

"*I want my wife back*," he said, surprised at the ferocity of his response. "I didn't bargain for mumus and waddling and expansion pants and having to cringe when some lard-assed tub of an individual comes hoving into view at a screening – *blimping* into view – and I'm forced to introduce her as my wife."

The woman absorbed this last as if it were a blow and then got up from her chair.

"I don't think I can go on like this," she said.

"You felt confident that you could."

"I was wrong. Clearly, it's impossible to treat someone . . ."

"When there's a dual connection," he said, finishing the thought. "I know."

They looked at each other in silence. He was the first to speak.

"What do we do?"

"Go on, I guess. We do love each other."

"We do," he said, putting his arms around her, the bulk of her and pressing her to him with all his strength. "Oh God, do we ever."

Fit As a Fiddle

IT WAS A DARK TIME FOR DUGAN. Though he was hale, if not hearty, at sixty-two, his friends were dropping like flies. First to go had been O'Shea who had found the strains of a divorce to be unbearable and waded into a pond in Patchogue, never again to surface. Next came Taggert, a trumpet player who had been hospitalized with frail lungs, then quickly released when he set a record for blowing up pulmonary balloons. Yet soon after, he expired all the same – in a commercial hotel, surrounded by weeping jazz musicians. No sooner had Dugan recovered from this loss than he received word that Lieberman, his long-time editor, had keeled over at his desk, as if he had grown weary of reading introspective first novels. Lieberman had been Dugan's age, almost to the day, and had appeared to be strong as an ox. Brilliant at shoring up defective manuscripts, he had imposed a clever structure on Dugan's complex study of nineteenth-century Balkan cabals. The loss was a grievous one to Dugan who could not help but think – it's getting closer.

Perhaps it was a cycle. He had heard that such losses came in threes. But that theory was blasted out of the water when he received a call from his psychiatrist's wife saying that Dr. Werner had been taken by pneumonia – and as a result, Dugan's Wednesday afternoon session had been canceled. Dugan expressed his condolences – no finer man had ever walked the earth, etc – but in truth, he was angry at Werner. At their last session, the doctor had produced a reference work of distinguished historians that failed to list Dugan's name. Thoughtlessly, and perhaps because of his advancing years, Werner, in referring to Dugan's work, had used the term "intermediate." Dugan was crushed. At the end of the hour, he had raced to the library and searched out reference books in which his name *was* listed – but now he would never get to brandish them at Werner. The widow gave Dugan the name of another man he could see, but although Dugan dutifully scribbled down the phone number, he knew he would never use it. Werner was the second psychiatrist who had dropped dead on him; he had lost faith in the profession.

Dugan hoped for a let-up in the parade of grim developments, but none came. Soon after, he was notified by fax that Smiley, the owner of his favorite saloon, had died in the back room of the popular watering place. In this case, the news came as no surprise. Not only was Smiley a heavy drinker, there was also a drug habit that was supposed to be a secret but that everyone in the world knew about. In Dugan's dwindling circle, the concern was not so much for poor Smiley – but whether the saloon could function without him. And before Dugan knew what hit him, he lost his accountant, who was barely fifty – although he did smoke a great many cigars. Dugan had given some thought to firing Esposito – who never really understood the peculiarities of artists – but fortunately the accountant died before Dugan could let him go.

He looked on with dismay as friend after friend bit the dust. And if that wasn't bad enough, even his enemies started to go under. Chief among them was Toileau who had accused him in print of shoddy research on his massive Bismarck biography – an attack so vicious and unfair it took Dugan a decade to regain his confidence. He had hated Toileau – how could he not? – but the man was, after all, a contemporary – and it was only small consolation that the nit-picking critic was safely in his grave.

Despite the circling ring of doom, Dugan saw no other course than to press on. After all, wasn't his favorite hero Marshall Joseph Joffre, whose answer to every battlefield situation, no matter how dire, was "J'attaque."

Dugan lived in the country where he had carefully surrounded himself with youth – a wife who was twenty years his junior, an adopted son of twelve, and young dogs. In truth, his wife took fourteen kinds of pills to make sure her disposition was cheery. But his son excelled in ice hockey and could lift Dugan off the ground. Dugan was not particularly hypochondriacal, although an occasional twinge in his chest got him nervous. But to be on the safe side, he wolfed down fresh vegetables and made sure not to eat anything he enjoyed too much. His one exception was the large pair of greasy egg rolls he treated himself to on his occasional forays into Manhattan. The hell with it, he told himself, as he took a seat at the bar of *Ho's*. I've got to have something.

At the moment, he was working on a DeGaulle biography (the youthful DeGaulle, of course). It troubled him that Lieberman hadn't trained a skilled underling to take over as Dugan's editor. But he forged ahead all the same. His routine was to lose himself in the book for two weeks, then come up for air with a drive to the city and lunch with a friend. But even his surviving friends weren't setting the world on fire. His choice of lunch companions included Burke, a poet who had been fitted up with a pig's bladder, Karen Armstrong, a brilliant copywriter whose leg had been chopped off to stem a circulatory ailment, and Ellis, the healthiest of them all, a jade collector who wore a pacemaker and had a penile implant. Another candidate was Grebs, his former attorney, who had been in and out of mental institutions. In this case, he could imagine the repartee: "They've suggested volts, Dugan. How shall I instruct them?"

His friends were all fine, upstanding individuals, each one a credit to his or her profession – but Dugan lacked the courage to meet them for lunch. Considering the circumstances, how could he be expected to concentrate on food. So on his trips to the city, he ate alone, checked a few bookstores and drove home in cowardice.

An argument could be made that the condition of his friends had nothing to do with Dugan – there were healthy people all over the place. A case in point was his brother Kevin, the picture of wood-cutting vigor in far-off Maine. But Dugan didn't buy the argument. The numbers were against him. The wagons were circling. Even Kevin had begun to send him childhood mementoes, explaining that at sixty-five, it was time to "pare down his life a bit."

Dugan's one consolation was that of all the friends he had lost, there wasn't one who had a claim on his heart – someone he could call in the middle of the night for a discussion of his darkest fears – of death, for example. Could he survive the loss of such an individual? And then one day he found out, when he learned that Enzo Cavalucci had lost a secret and uncomplaining battle with Mehlman's Syndrome, something new, a spin-off of Alzheimer's. (Cavalucci had once joked that it was unwise to catch a disease that had someone's name attached to it.) When Dugan received the news from Cavalucci's mistress, he wept into the phone without shame. And when Cavalucci's widow called later to confirm, he wept again. He had loved his friend, but hadn't realized to what extent – until it was too late. A rival historian, Cavalucci had enjoyed far greater eminence than Dugan and had even sold his Boer War trilogy to the movies. Cavalucci had gotten rich, but such was Dugan's love for the man that he hadn't begrudged him a dime. At a troubled time of his life, Dugan had set out with a lead pipe to kill his first wife's lover; it was Cavalucci who had gently stayed his hand, saying "You don't want to do that." Actually, Dugan did want to do it, but that wasn't the point. Cavalucci had rescued him from a potential shitstorm. On another occasion, sensing Dugan was in financial difficulty, Cavalucci had wired him $10,000, along with a note saying there was no rush to pay it back. And if he needed another ten, that could be arranged, too. Dugan barely slept until he had settled the debt, but he never forgot his friend's kindness. And when Dugan's Bismarck bio had been raked over the coals, it was Cavalucci who stood up bravely at a gathering of historians and recited selections from the work – focusing on the ones that had suffered the greatest abuse. Cavalucci lived in St. Louis. The two men rarely saw each other, but they spoke regularly on the phone, each conversation picking up seamlessly from the last. Of late, Dugan had noticed a tendency on Cavalucci's part to lose his focus on the phone, but he attributed that to a preoccupation with his planned Cardinal Richelieu masterwork.

In the weeks that followed Cavalucci's passing, Dugan was inconsolable, and could think of nothing else. Acquaintances were one thing – but the loss of this wise and friendly bear of a man – a rock he could always cling to – was more than he could stand. Dugan's wife, an independent woman who dabbled in the sale of waterfront property, barely noticed his extended grief. For the time being, Dugan slept in the guest room, which she didn't notice either. His son trailed him around, hoping his father's melancholy would pass, then gave up and went outdoors to jump up and down on a lonely trampoline. Work was no longer Dugan's salvation. How was he supposed to get excited about DeGaulle's childhood? He sat at his desk, mindlessly reciting the phone number of his boyhood apartment in Jackson Heights, reflecting on his parents, his brothers and sisters, all of them gone except Kevin who was making preparations to join them.

One day, unaccountably, his spirits came awake. Momentarily cheerful, he reached into his pocket to pay for gas at a service station and pulled out an expensive goatskin credit card holder – a gift from Cavalucci. The sight of it put him right back where he started. At the fish store, the following morning, a woman he barely knew gave him an update on her husband's condition in a nursing home. "Mel's incontinent," she shouted across the shellfish counter. He returned home with his flounder fillets in time to receive a call from the representative of a family of blind Hispanics who had all been fired from their basket-weaving jobs on the eve of Thanksgiving. Before the man could ask for financial assistance, Dugan, to his everlasting shame, shouted into the phone.

"I can't take any more of this. Speak to my wife."

On that note, he packed an over-the-shoulder carry-all bag with pajamas, underwear, toiletries and a Helmuth Von Moltke memoir he planned to finish reading, no matter what. Then he drove to the hospital, although in truth, it was so close to his house that he could have walked. Of late, his wife had hinted that she'd had her fill of small town intrigue and wouldn't mind moving back to the city. Normally, Dugan gave in to her every whim. But on this occasion, he stalled and failed to list the house with a broker. He loved his spacious Colonial which was in such sharp contrast to the cramped apartment he had lived in as a boy. Also, he enjoyed the proximity of the hospital. In the winter months particularly, when the chic vacationers were partying in the city, he had the facility virtually to himself.

Dugan took a seat in the waiting room and was alone, except for a bartender who had suffered a clamming injury on his day off. When Dugan's name was called, he flashed a Fast-Track card and was whisked right through to a preliminary examining room where a nurse silently recorded his temperature and blood pressure.

As luck would have it, the doctor on call was Alvin Murdoch, Dugan's own physician, who had recently moved to the community, quickly attracting a strong following among the locals. Murdoch had once stopped Dugan outside the post office and gotten him to sign a petition having to do with encroaching health providers. It probably made sense, but Dugan felt he had been bullied into putting his name on it and had mistrusted Murdoch ever since. But the doctor had a reputation for thoroughness and it was difficult to get an appointment with him – so Dugan stayed on as a patient.

Murdoch checked the nurse's findings, then called up the results of Dugan's recent physical on the computer. He made some notes, then crossed his legs daintily, folded his hands on his knees and flashed the boyish smile that everyone except Dugan had found engaging.

"You *look* great. What's wrong?"

"Not a thing," said Dugan. "Actually, I'm fit as a fiddle. But as we both know, it's just a matter of time. So I thought I might as well check in and get an early start."

Neck and Neck

ALBERT P. WIENER. The mention of his name hadn't always made Baum sick with envy. Weiner was a few years his senior, but the two had started out neck and neck in the literary world. Wiener had published a *bildungsroman* which was praised for its intellectual reach, although several critics found it "bloated." Baum agreed, but felt that Wiener's skills were undeniable. Baum himself had written a book of stories – fables, really – that were admired by reviewers for their inventiveness and concision. Both Wiener and Baum were cited by the Frederick Buchner Foundation as two of the most promising artists of the Post-World War Two era.

Baum met Wiener for the first time at a literary cocktail party in Cologne. The tall and hawk-nosed Wiener told Baum: "You are on the cusp of something."

"As you are, too," said the shorter and more compactly built Baum, somewhat awkwardly.

For the next decade, both artists followed a similar path – publishing books and stories and essays that, for the most part, were warmly received. Wiener was shortlisted for the distinguished Gechwisterlein Award. Baum actually won the only slightly less esteemed Frankel/Sagner Prize for yet another volume of his finely crafted fables.

At this point, their careers – or literary lives – took divergent paths. Weiner, known to be a ladies man, moved from Cologne to Paris where he dated film stars who were slightly below the top tier. He wrote a racy account of his affair with one of them. She fired back with a scandalous version of her own that focused on Wiener's sexual inadequacies. Both accounts sold well.

Baum moved his family – his wife and two daughters – to Rome. No sooner had they arrived than Elmira Krantz Baum fell in love with a distributor of spaghetti westerns. She asked for and was granted a divorce. Though one of his daughters remained loyal to him, Baum was shattered by the breakup and turned to drugs and alcohol. Somehow he gathered his resources to write what many considered his best work – an unmistakably autobiographical novel about the breakup of his marriage. Following this small triumph, Baum, in a literary sense, began to tread water. He fell into an easy life as a translator of American film scripts for the Italian audience. His career took a surprising turn when he showed some skill as a director of screwball comedies, also designed for the Italian market. The money – always cash – was substantial – and the work was far from strenuous. His furnished apartment was luxurious. He enticed women with fast cars and cocaine. A few of his lovers may have found him appealing. He would never know. Apart from his dark and unsettled spirits at dawn, he led a comfortable, somewhat pampered life, one he felt he deserved after a harrowing and bitter marriage. It was his plan to return, at some distant point, to more "serious" pursuits. And he kept Wiener in his sights. His competitor – and that's how Baum thought of him – had written two huge essayistic novels, both of which grappled with eternal questions – who are we? – why are we here? Both works met with respect in small literary journals – though some felt that the books were little more than homages to Thomas Mann. Still, Baum admired Wiener for sticking to his last, while he, Baum, worked below his capabilities. Or so he thought. Nonetheless, Baum felt confident that he could "overtake" the man he thought of as his rival – or at least draw even with him in terms of literary achievement. All he had to do was close the door on his sybaritic life and step on the gas.

The two men had a single exchange by mail. Baum's letter was innocuous. He congratulated Wiener on one of his ponderous novels, which he had only skimmed. Wiener's response was to chastise Baum for falling into a trap of easy money.

"Why do you waste your time on movies? All that counts is the novel. Nothing else. *Nada, Nada, Nada.*"

Baum's reaction was dismissive. He told a colleague: "One *Nada* would have been sufficient."

The two men met once again, by chance, on the Piazza della Republica. Wiener was in Rome to attend a literary seminar. Baum, who hadn't been invited, was walking off a night of strenuous carousing. He wore dark glasses and a Stetson to cover the evidence of his dissolute behavior.

The sharp-eyed Wiener saw through the disguise. Full of good cheer, he called out: "Baum! Why are you hiding?"

Wiener then reached out and tipped Baum's hat backward. Baum was offended and clenched his fists as if to strike a blow. But he had no strength. The debauched night had stolen his energy. He clamped the hat back on his head, waved a disgusted arm and slouched away. Wiener, who missed nothing, had sensed Baum's weakness and jumped on the chance to assert his superiority, to treat the other man with contempt. Baum took note of the offensive gesture and vowed never to be caught again in a depleted and whorish state. He quickly forgot the vow.

In the years that followed, both men stayed below the literary waves, while young lions fought to take their place. Wiener traveled far afield with two books on modern architecture. Neither was a threat to Baum who felt, along with at least one distinguished critic, that Wiener had gotten in over his head.

Along with his lowly cinematic function, Baum became an unofficial "greeter" in Rome, taking visiting luminaries on a tour of the city's fleshpots. He kept a toe in the literary waters, although just barely, with an amusing tourist guidebook to the Eternal City. One visitor to Rome was a distinguished film director from Sweden. He told Baum that he had worked with Wiener on a screenplay.

"It was in Stockholm. We were together in a hotel for four long months. We almost drove each other crazy, but we couldn't pull it off."

"That's hard to believe," said Baum. "Wiener ridiculed such work and swore he'd have nothing to do with it.

"Still," said Baum, on reflection. "I always *knew* he'd attempt a screenplay, if only in stealth."

Shortly before his sixtieth birthday Baum said goodbye to the film colony and left Rome. He moved back to Cologne, determined finally to address his "serious" work. In truth, he was no longer quite clear as to what it was. He thought he'd begin with God and the Universe and take it from there. No sooner had he arrived than he met a young and pretty sociologist. Within a year, they were married and Magda had given birth to twin girls. Baum was delighted with this development. For the moment he thought little of the added financial strain.

He tried, unsuccessfully, to get up some traction on a novel, but he'd taken too long a vacation from literature and had no feel for it. He'd heard that Tennessee Williams, in his late years, had scribbled notes in Gaelic to bartenders, saying "I have lost my way."

If the great playwright could lose his way, why not Baum?

In search of safe ground, Baum tried a few plays of his own. Theatre owners seduced him, then turned away without explanation. What began as an innocent dalliance with the stage cost him the better part of a decade.

Baum was approaching seventy now. All he had to show for his recent efforts was an article on hormones in a Swedish health magazine. He consoled himself with the knowledge that great men such as Goethe and Cervantes had produced important work in their late years. He began to regret the wastrel time in Rome, but not entirely. Though he was beginning to drown in debt, his excellent wife, Magda, was supportive. "Those years you spent in Rome – they weren't wasted – they all went into the soup."

"Maybe so," said Baum, "but where's the soup?"

Mercifully, Wiener hadn't been heard from for some time. It was as if he was unwilling to take advantage of the plodding and unproductive Baum. Then, treacherously, Wiener exploded on the literary world with a 1000-page Holocaust novel. It was told from the point of view of a wily Jewish tailor who had survived for five years in the center of wartime Berlin, all the while making slacks for the Nazis. Before this publication, Wiener and Baum, as if by tacit agreement, had avoided the Ultimate Subject. Both Jews, though not practicing, they had fallen in with Eli Weisel's view that the magnitude of the Holocaust demanded literary silence. Baum felt, and assumed Wiener agreed, that the genocide existed in another dimension. The very mention of it, like God's name, was a crime. To approach it with cheap art – or even decent art – was to spit on it. In violation of this silent compact, Wiener had plunged ahead all the same and produced his thunderbolt. The effect was to electrify the literary world . . . Suddenly, there wasn't a newspaper or magazine, popular or otherwise, that didn't feature a Weiner interview, a lengthy critique not only of his current work but of his entire oeuvre. The man was in Baum's face from dawn to dusk. His books sold by the truckload. Television might as well have been called *All Wiener All the Time*. No sooner had the Wiener craze died down than a revisionist attack took hold. Its substance was that Wiener had been overrated. Heavy-handedly, a tabloid cried out: *Wiener's Back, But Where's the Schnitzel?* The attacks gave solace to Baum, but only temporarily. They kept the flame alive. New and passionate defenders of Wiener found their voices. Baum had acknowledged for some time that Wiener had outdistanced him by a considerable margin. But at least Baum could make out his silhouette on the horizon. Now, he no longer saw his nemesis, only a disappearing puff of greatness.

The effect of the Wiener phenomenon on Baum was literary paralysis. Obviously, Wiener's triumph was not directed at Baum specifically, but it might as well have been. Now and then, a critic would mention Baum's name in connection with the Sixties. Inevitably – and sickeningly – the writer would point out that at one time, Baum had been mentioned "in the same breath" as Albert Wiener.

Baum tried to go back to his early fables, but there was no passion in his efforts. I.B. Singer, the Nobelist, had written: "Just because a man has written ten good novels, it doesn't mean the next one won't be trash."

Baum found strength in this observation. But where were his ten good ones?

In an hour-length television interview, Wiener was seen in a spare and gloomy apartment with a rowing machine. For the most part, he lived alone and continued to date fading actresses. What kind of life was that? Baum told himself that at least he experienced the joys of family. But in truth, Magda Baum had become fat and indolent. One daughter was a survivalist in the state of Washington. Another drew listless watercolors in Trondheim. The twins lived at home in a state of romantic confusion, dating half the young men of Cologne.

Was it possible that Wiener was better off with his fading actresses and his rowing machine?

Despairingly, Baum abandoned his literary efforts and found a job at a community college as a teacher of creative writing.

"If I can reach only one or two young minds," he heard himself say, self-importantly, in the faculty lunch room. . . . "If I can only pass on what I know. . . ."

But what did he know? Envy of another writer? One that he had underestimated? Is this what he wanted to pass on to young minds?

One morning, Baum opened a newspaper and read that Wiener had suffered ("been felled by") a stroke. To his everlasting shame and humiliation, Baum took heart in the news. Still, he felt it only right to extend his sympathies. After all, this was a fellow craftsman. He called an agent in Vienna who had once represented Wiener – and Baum as well.

"I heard about Wiener," he said. "Tragic."

"It's not so tragic," the agent said. "If you or I had a stroke, God forbid, it would be one thing. But he has entire medical teams, the finest in Europe, attending to him. Round-the-clock nurses are at his disposal. He'll survive beautifully. . . . And by the way, what have you been doing?."

"I keep busy," said Baum, vaguely.

"You were as good as Wiener. Yet look what he's achieved. And you. . . ."

Here he sighed hopelessly.

Baum longed to fire back. Where are the Wiener movies? The short fiction? And where is his family? Where is his life?

But the questions lacked force. He choked back his words.

After three months of recuperative silence, Wiener returned to the literary wars, as if the stroke had given him added strength. . . . In the months and years that followed he was more productive than ever. First came a slyly crafted novella about adultery. (When did he have time to write it? Had he tossed it off in intensive care?) This was followed by an announcement that a new play by Wiener on Life, Death and the Universe (Baum's themes?) was to be produced as part of the Theatretreffen Berlin Festival. The play was thrown immediately into production. Baum waited tensely for the reviews, which were tepid. "The Great Man Stumbles . . ." said one. No sooner had Baum taken a grateful breath then it was announced that Albert Wiener's play would be mounted in a grand production in Petersburg.

"Here we will do it properly," said the Russian impresario.

En route to attend rehearsals, Wiener announced to the press that he had signed a contract with the Pflaume/Kunstler Presse to do the first revisionist biography of Benjamin Disraeli. This was yet another venture that Baum had thought wistfully of tackling. Wiener had already completed four hundred pages. The rest was in meticulously organized notes.

Each mention of Wiener's name or one of his projects was like a spear lodged in Baum's side. Only on those rare days when his rival was absent from the news was Baum able to draw a clean breath. In mid-semester, he gave up his teaching job. "I'm not worthy of it," he told the headmaster, and tossed his classroom keys on the man's desk.

The following day Baum experienced a *coup d'age*. Virtually overnight, he became short of breath and developed roving stomach pains. His knees swelled to twice their size. A doctor reported that he had lost an inch and a half in height. He walked with two canes and was easily jostled in crowds.

Baum attributed this sudden decline to a single item of gossip in *Bunte Illustrierte*. Wiener was reported to be dating Lotte Frietag, a blonde and exquisite nineteen-year-old who was a rising star of the German cinema. There was a grainy photograph of the couple in matching bikinis, "frolicking" on the beach in St. Tropez. Though Wiener had a modest paunch, he looked surprisingly well-toned. He had, of course, enjoyed a glittering career. For him to possess the ravishing Frietag as well was unconscionable. Baum imagined himself saying to his rival: "Wiener, you go too far."

Baum followed his wife's advice; the couple moved to a small village outside of Schwernitz, where he would no longer be caught up in the turmoil of city life. The twins rented an apartment in Berlin, sponsored by the dwindling residuals of Baum's Italian film career.

"You lived a wild life," said one. "Why shouldn't we?"

In the years that followed, Wiener continued to produce books at an infuriating pace. Even a wild novelistic foray into science fiction was bought by the films.

"What I have in mind," said the director who had been assigned to Wiener's project, "is a grand trilogy that will be faithful to the master."

A single heartening note – from Baum's point of view – was that Wiener and the exquisite Lotte Frietag had agreed to separate and to remain good friends. But this, too, was taken away.

"I finally realized" she told a tabloid interviewer "that it was only the sex that kept us bound together. The man was voracious. I could no longer keep pace."

For his part, the white-haired Baum followed the same routine each day: he rose early, spent as much time as possible with his breakfast and the newspapers, then took a nap. When he awakened, he walked – or rather trudged – up a little hill to a shed he referred to as his "office." There, he reviewed notes for works that he had set aside. Why push on with them when he could never catch sight of Wiener, much less draw abreast of him. It crossed his mind that a single small classic might do the trick – but *Candide* had already been written. After making a feeble and fruitless pass at a new venture, he reread the fables he had written as a young man. Then he called it a day.

And then one morning, as he prepared a tasteless but healthful breakfast of oatmeal and berries, he glanced at the newspaper. A banner headline announced the death of the great novelist Albert P. Weiner. The man who, perhaps unknowingly, had caused Baum such enormous grief, had succumbed to pancreatic failure at the University Hospital of Innsbruck. The obituary was lengthy. It seemed to Baum that it went on forever. At one point, the author threw in a bitter personal note.

"One of the great literary crimes of the century is that Albert P. Wiener – obviously for political reasons – was denied the Nobel Prize for Literature."

Baum wondered about his own obituary. How much space would be allotted to him? Was there any assurance that he would receive more than a brief mention? And would those damnable words – he'd once been "mentioned in the same breath as Wiener" – be repeated?

A small funeral was scheduled for friends and family, to be followed, weeks later, by a large memorial service for the general public. It seemed unlikely that Baum would be asked to attend the funeral. He made a vague plan to show up at the memorial service and scribbled down some notes, in case he was asked to speak.

"An unlikely giant has left us," he would begin.

But why 'unlikely?'

Baum's eighty-ninth birthday was a week away. After reading the Wiener obituary, he finished his breakfast and took what had now become a long and arduous trek to the shed. Once there, he started an excellent woodfire. In past years, with nothing better to do, he had become an expert on kindling. With some effort, he took his old Remington portable typewriter down from the top shelf of a closet. His daughters had ridiculed him for not switching to a computer, but for many years, he'd felt he had no use for either machine. Sitting at his desk, he blew on his twisted fingers to try to get some blood flowing. His back ached and he could feel his breakfast, undigested, in what felt like a package beneath his ribs. Simple breathing was a hardship. Only one eye functioned properly. But Wiener was gone. Now he could focus. Now he could begin.

A Pebble In
His Shoe

THE HOTEL, in the south of France, was Egyptian in motif and baffling in its design, as if the architect had proceeded with his first draft and been wildly off target. Corridors that seemed intriguing suddenly turned dark and came to an abrupt ending. The bar was out on a weird limb. Only with luck could Jack find his room without assistance. At first, he took on some of the responsibility for his confusion, assuming that the hotel was probably brilliant in its conception and it was his fault for not getting the hang of it. He then learned that a group of Lebanese had lost millions on its wild and purposeless construction and had finally thrown up their hands and sold it back to the French at enormous loss. The new owners, offering immaculate service, caviar and fresh croissants, were inching their way toward a profit.

He had come to France for some talks with a film actor he admired named Marty Hatcher. Brilliant in his career in England, Hatcher had performed adequately in American films and had gotten rich. He continued to be brilliant in flashes, and it was the flashes that Jack remembered – a lopsided smile, a ridiculous walk, the perfect mispronunciation of a familiar word. Which was not why Jack made the trip. A French producer had paid for it; considerable sums would come Jack's way if the proposed film got off the ground.

A nice bonus was that he liked Hatcher, although their first meeting had begun ominously. Much like the design of Jack's hotel, the notion he proposed to Hatcher had been wildly off target. Jack saw himself as having made a wasted trip and fell into general despair. In this situation, another star might have been cruel and let him flounder. But Hatcher had gently eased him onto safe and comfortable ground. In essence, what they would do was keep the outlines of Jack's idea and drop the politics (an irritant to the non-political Hatcher). And they would, of course, hold on to the fun. They had been dining at a four-star restaurant with Hatcher's fourth wife, a lovely woman named Hillary who had to be some three decades or more younger than the sixtyish film star. It was only when Hatcher had pushed aside the crisis that Jack felt able to take his first deep, satisfied breath. The days that followed were cozy and peaceful – cool, off-season nights, light work, ripe local wines, the three of them taking trips to inspect the seaside house that Hatcher was having built in a nearby village. Portuguese construction men with fat hands lovingly shaped the new beams.

All of this pleasure in spite of the fact that their group was off-balance. Jack was alone. They had each other. Hatcher's wife had a perfect face and wide, astonished eyes. It was as if amazing stories were continually being whispered in her ear. Hillary drove them about in a Ferrari at hair-raising speeds. Jack assumed she was a good driver, although her success depended upon everyone else, pedestrians and other drivers, playing their parts to perfection. She had done a few small roles in films, her specialty being young girls bewildered by first love. But she did not have the usual starlet background. Her father had been a naturalist of some prominence and her mother, a novelist, had once been shortlisted for the Booker Prize.

There was an instant connection between Hillary and Jack, but he chose, if not to ignore it, to finesse it. At the end of the evening, when they were lightly and happily drunk on wine, the three of them would stand and hug one another, a three-way embrace. Then Jack would return to his hotel to think about Hatcher and wonder about Hillary, though not to covet her. He was alone, but he did not feel in the least bit lonely. As long as the visit did not go on and on.

While their new house was being built, Hatcher and his wife
had rented a villa some five hundred yards from Jack's puzzle of
a hotel. The actor, who had suffered a stroke, liked to sleep late
and to begin work at noon. Since Jack rose early, at least in foreign
countries, that left him with the morning to kill. He took fresh
walks through a nearby forest area, trying to ignore the giant pa-
trolling dogs of a breed he had never encountered, then fingered
merchandise in the port area; after breakfast, he sat out on the
wharf, putting his face up to the sun. Out of the corner of his
eyes, he watched fishermen making operatically hostile gestures
at one another – any one of which would have caused instant
death in the city in which Jack had lived. But these raucous com-
batants were friends and generally walked off arm in arm.
Promptly at noon, Jack would appear at Hatcher's villa, generally
to find that the actor had not arisen. Hillary would flash by in a
robe, legs exposed, apologetically running her hands through
ringlets of golden hair. Hatcher would appear soon after, also in a
robe, dazed, flushed, also apologetic, and begin to imitate Frenchmen for Jack, as an offering for his being late. That was the extent
of their work, Hatcher doing imitations of eccentrics he wanted to
work into the movie – spinsters, mad Englishmen, adenoidal
Frenchmen, doddering old white colonials. He would do them
into a German-made tape recorder, one of several dozen he had
placed around the house, the idea being that Jack would take the
cassettes back to the States, to be referred to, while he did the
work. Hatcher would simply break into these imitations, taking
no time at all to prepare or to get into character. This was a phenomenon to Jack, more so than the brilliance of the imitations. Often, he wondered if Hatcher had any real character of his own,
other than to be sweet and befuddled.

One day, at noon, Jack let himself into the villa and sensed
an unusual stillness in the air. Since the work was casual, you
could not say that he and Hatcher were at any critical juncture in
the project. They had a strong middle section, so it did not seem
terribly important that they did not have a precise beginning

and lacked a payoff. They would get it. After half an hour or so during which neither Hatcher nor Hillary tumbled out in a robe, Jack, somewhat shy about doing so, shouted out: "Anyone home?"

Hillary came out to greet him, shaken, as if someone had told her a fairy tale with a horrible ending.

"Is anything wrong?" Jack asked, idiotically, since it was plain that something was.

"Marty's had a terrible row with Ian St. Clair," said Hillary, barely able to get out the word. Jack recognized the name Ian St. Clair as that of a young financial wizard who had saved troubled rock groups from insolvency and now served as Hatcher's representative.

Hatcher soon appeared, the color gone from his face, his dressing gown dipping low and revealing what might have been the start of a woman's breasts. In the ensuing hour, calls and cables went back and forth to London. In bits and pieces, Jack learned that Hatcher had balked at proceeding with several of St. Clair's recommended projects. Somewhere along the line, the financial adviser had suggested that Hillary had been interfering in Hatcher's life. St. Clair had actually gotten her on the phone and berated her.

"I believe he called you a cunt, didn't he, darling?" said Hatcher mildly, after the last of the calls.

"How can he say that?" Hillary had responded, her lips trembling.

She turned to Jack, distraught, and said, "I've been modest in my suggestions – and everything I've done has been to shore up my husband."

"There, there," said Hatcher, covering his wife's hands with his own. "We'll get it straightened out, don't you worry. Ian doesn't know diddly about creative affairs."

Jack listened to all of this and found it incomprehensible that a financial adviser would berate a client's wife.

"Listen," he said, "this is none of my business, but I'm *making* it my business. The idea of a financial person uttering a single *word* about your private life . . ."

He became so choked up with anger that he was forced to stop and collect himself.

"You don't know Ian," said Hatcher despairingly.

"I don't have to," said Jack. "I know all about him from what you've told me."

"We're locked together in a hundred situations," said Hatcher. "I can't very well just dump all of my affairs on someone else's desk. I'd be ruined."

"I don't care how brilliant he is," said Jack. "There are other brilliant people. By six o'clock tonight, you can have a line of them circling your house. And they won't have a word to say about your wife."

"You know," said Hatcher to Hillary. "I believe old Jack here may be on to something?"

Taking Hillary by the hand, he disappeared into the study. After ten minutes or so, Hillary appeared, the tears erased. Handing Jack a cassette, she said, "This is Marty's response to Ian."

Jack slipped it into a cassette player and heard the following, in the voice of the famed comedian.

"My dear Ian. Stop. My wife is an utter delight. Stop. She has only been a comfort to me. Stop. If Hillary is hurting me, then the Queen Mother is a dyke. Stop. Why are you trying to spoil our fine relationship of five years? Stop. Your totally confused friend. Stop. Marty.

"It's quite forceful, don't you feel?" said Hillary.

"Can we take a drive?" said Jack.

By late afternoon, some of the color had come back into Hatcher's face. Emerging from his study, he broke into an imitation of an aging third-rate French nightclub singer, moving through imaginary ringside tables on flat feet, with microphone in hand. It was quite heartbreaking. The three of them drove out to a favorite local vineyard, Hatcher at the wheel, Hillary uncharacteristically at his side, as if the film star had arrived at some confident new truth in his life. By silent agreement, it was decided that they would discontinue the work for the time being. Jack would gather up the tapes, return to the States, work on the script and return in a couple of months with a first draft. That night, they went to a legendary French restaurant with amazingly tall waiters. After a highly satisfactory dinner, Hatcher asked one of them if he could sniff the bouquet of all the fruit brandies.

"And perhaps a shoe if you've got a loose one about."

The brandies were presented by an unflappable waiter, but not the shoe. All of this fell short of being hysterically funny, but indicated to Jack that his friend may at least have come out of the woods.

"I'm sorry you had to be subjected to all that unpleasantness," said Hatcher.

"I was only concerned about you," said Jack.

Outside, what appeared to be a whole season's worth of rain suddenly came down. Hatcher insisted on going to get the car, more evidence of returning vigor. Jack and Hillary waited beneath an awning. Almost imperceptibly, she moved her hair against his face. He tried to ignore this. In the car, she said: "I was only doing what I felt a wife should do. Marty's wife, your wife, Jack, anyone's wife."

"I don't relish the prospect," said Hatcher, not hearing this, "but I'm afraid I'll have to go to London tomorrow and thrash this out with Ian."

At the villa, they said a quick goodbye. Jack was always more brisk in these situations than his heart wanted him to be. He would have to get around to correcting that. He kissed Hillary on the cheek and she offered her other cheek as well. He started to hug Hatcher, who moved forward as if to return the expected embrace. But they both drew back and settled for claps on the back and a good handshake.

"I'll see you in a month or so," said Jack. "Thanks for the many kindnesses."

"Be well, dear boy," said Hatcher.

It was Jack's daughter who told him the news. She met him at the airport and they decided to have dinner in town, jet lag or no jet lag.

"Have you heard about Mr. Hatcher?" she asked. She was a quiet girl who always looked at him out of the corner of her eye. She was sixteen, lived with her mother, and kept a key to Jack's apartment.

"He had some kind of attack," she said. "It was on the six o'clock news."

Back at his apartment, Jack called his French producer, who was a giggler, and who reported the following information: While en route to London, Marty Hatcher had suffered an attack of food poisoning. The doctors were not taking any chances. Considering the actor's history of poor health, they had taken him to Charing Cross Hospital for observation. (The French producer even worked a giggle into this conversation.)

Jack went ahead and had dinner with his daughter.

"I saw it coming," he said and told her the story of Hatcher and the financial adviser.

"Maybe it's cheap psychology, but he did not want to go to that meeting with St. Clair. He was afraid of him, and, either consciously or not, he got himself good and sick so he could avoid it."

Jack's daughter wanted to hear Hatcher on the cassettes; at his apartment, they listened to the actor do a demented English schoolteacher, a mad archaeologist who'd been lost in the jungle, and an Hispanic drug dealer. (This last was off by a hair.) That night, Jack worried about Hatcher and had to admit to himself that he was concerned about their project as well. Did that make him a selfish individual?

The food poisoning turned out to be a cover story designed to mask a serious heart attack. Hatcher died the next day. It was apparently not the first heart attack; the actor had been secretly wearing a pacemaker. The death received a huge amount of press coverage, which pleased Jack, who had been disappointed when the food poisoning got only a few lines in the press. He had all kinds of thoughts. The wildest and most presumptuous one had to do with whether Hatcher, on his deathbed, had willed him something – a piece of sensitive high-tech recording equipment, for example. He was glad that he had attacked the guru financier. What he was sorriest about was that he hadn't gone ahead and given Hatcher the farewell hug. He talked to his daughter about Hatcher a lot.

"You couldn't make it stick in a normal court," he said, "but that son of a bitch St. Clair is guilty of murder. I run into that more and more in Hollywood, some bean counter telling me how to tell a story. And this is where it can lead."

He thought of flying to London and confronting St. Clair with the accusation, but he knew he never would. Though he considered himself a moral man, he was aware that he lacked a moral follow-through. The film project, of course, foundered. No one who was available could quite fill Hatcher's shoes. There was some talk of the great Vittorio Gassman, but it would have meant starting from scratch, and Jack had no heart to do so. The French producer paid him half the money that was due – a fairly honorable gesture as these things go.

Jack was not astonished when Hillary called from London after several weeks and said that she and her mother were going to be visiting the States and could they all get together. Jack felt a buzzing in his legs as he talked to her and said of course, yes. She arrived without her mother. And she brought along the news that she was being considered for a role in a major film that would feature several international stars. All were on the level of Maximilian Schell, who had already been signed. Hillary had gained some weight and was now hopelessly beautiful. Other than to say it was awful, they did not discuss Hatcher. There didn't seem to be much more to be said. Jack took her to his apartment, which was somewhat lavish, at least in size. He quickly explained that it had been leased for him as part of a film deal. They had never kissed before, but made love almost immediately, as if by pre-arrangement. He hadn't felt they were far enough along in their affair for this to happen, but she turned her back and did a slow, naked dance for him against the blinds. Of course, he made love to her again. She decided that night that she would give up acting, which had never interested her, and enroll in a graduate course in international law. And if it was all right with Jack, she would stay with him for a while. It was all right with Jack, although he had lived alone for several years and had to wonder if he would be able to function with someone in residence.

It worked out decently in some respects. Hillary turned out to be a magnificent cook, her specialization being the sauces of Provence. Part of his regimen had been an almost reflexive nightly visit to a saloon whose raffish following included writers, artists, film types, and the like. She became his companion on these visits, which soon tapered off. They stayed in much of the time, making love at a civilized pace until one of them picked up the tempo. He felt that it was Hillary. Though twenty years her senior, he managed, though barely, to keep stride.

Jack did not get much work done, although he played at it, putting in the requisite time, attacking a new project with his usual thoroughness. But he felt self-conscious all the while. There was a very large pebble in his shoe. One night, after he had finished going through the motions at his desk, he lay back on his recliner and his thoughts drifted to poor Hatcher, his brilliant improvisations, his drained and befuddled look as he emerged from his bedroom suite each day at noon. This in turn led him to reflect on Ian St. Clair, whose attempt to separate Hillary and Hatcher had, in Jack's view, sent the poor actor to his grave.

Hillary returned from class soon after and immediately came up behind him, smelling of the street, her hair brushing up against his cheek. She bit his earlobe gently, reminding him of her fierce and exquisite teeth.

"What's up?" he asked.

"Nothing, darling," she said. "I was wondering if you had any plans for the evening."

It occurred to him that they had made love that morning and the night before and in the afternoon of the previous day as well, when her class had been canceled. And, since she had moved in, on more occasions than he dared to remember.

Nonetheless, he got to his feet, took her appealingly damp hand, and wearily followed her into the bedroom, thinking that he had done Ian St. Clair a grave injustice.

The Thespian

YEARS BACK, when Harry had the Two Big Pictures and was considered (there was no other way to put this) a hot young Hollywood screenwriter – the interviewer at a Los Angeles radio station had asked him how and when he got his ideas. It was a nice soft pitch and Harry got some good wood on it. He said he read five newspapers in the morning, which was not only accurate but also guaranteed a "wow" or some other awed response. Harry said he also read *books* – a little dig here at his Hollywood colleagues, which probably didn't register. And he built on his personal experiences.

"But I only *build* on them," he said, throwing in a little charming self-deprecation, "since my life isn't all that fascinating."

Harry then said that his best ideas – and he used this as his capper – were the ones that came to him out of nowhere.

"They just land on my shoulder, like a butterfly."

No such idea had landed on Harry's shoulder for quite some time. He was waiting for one to land – or "alight" – he may have said "alight" – in a hotel in Miami when the call came through, offering him a small part in a movie (which he would later refer to as a "feature film").

The caller was an old – or make that *ex*-girlfriend – named Vera Landers. Harry had not heard from her in decades. Having felt rejected by New York (and possibly by Harry) Vera, who'd been the assistant editor of a magazine for the dry-cleaning trade, had moved to Los Angeles and reinvented herself as a screenwriter. Rising quickly through the ranks of what not only Charlton Heston, but Harry himself had once called "the industry," she had recently joined Jane Campion, Penny Marshall, Nora Ephron and a handful of others as a member of that elite group of women who got to write and direct their own movies.

"Why me?" asked Harry, after telling Vera how delighted he was to hear from her. He saw no need to point out that there were plenty of SAG members around who could use the work. "I'm no actor."

"You don't have to be," said Vera. "You just have to be yourself. You play the owner of a shop that specializes in rare books."

Setting aside the question of whether he wanted to do any acting at all, Harry saw immediately that he would be able to handle a role of that type. And at least she had not asked him to be a burned-out screenwriter, which he sort of was. But it had never even crossed his *mind* to be an actor. (Although, come to think of it, Robert Duvall – or someone who *looked* like Robert Duvall – an attractively chiseled bald guy – had once seen Harry climb out of the pool at the Beverly Hills Hotel and told him his face was meant for the Big Screen. Of course, that was twenty years back. And it may have been a gay thing.)

"Let me talk to my 'people'," said Harry, a little levity here, since it had been some time since he *had* any people. He had a feeling that Vera knew that.

"Terrific," said Vera, using that all-purpose Hollywood description for things terrific or not. "But don't take forever. And I'll fax you the sides."

"What was that all about?" asked Harry's fifteen-year-old daughter, who was spending part of her school break with him. She had been waiting to use the phone so she could tell people she had just gotten back from a school trip to Barcelona. Harry had taught Megan that the most important thing about going to places like Barcelona is that you get to tell people that you just got back from them. And she had learned her lessons well.

"Somebody offered me a part in a movie."

"Why?" she asked, somehow managing to squeeze two syllables out of one word, in the manner of teen actresses in the sitcoms that Harry denied watching.

Harry was disappointed by the question. Wasn't a daughter supposed to think her father could do anything? Every time Harry thought he had the hang of having a daughter, he was back at square one.

"They seem to think I'd be good at it."

Megan picked up the phone, then checked her hair in the mirror, as if she wanted to look good for the call she was about to make.

"How big a part is it?"

"I don't know," said Harry. "They're faxing me the sides."

"Sides?" she said. "You mean there's more than one?"

"It can be misleading. It might be just one side – and they send you the *surrounding* sides – so that you know what the movie is about."

"I'll bet it's big," said Megan after consideration. "And you've *got* to do it. If my friends found out you'd been offered a part in a movie and turned it *down*, they'd never forgive me."

"Then I guess that settles it," said Harry, letting the slight disjunction in logic go by.

"It's real little," said Megan, after a glance at the sides. She'd been reading *The Mill On The Floss*, a school assignment, and at the same time keeping one eye on the fax machine. "You have three lines and one of them is 'hi.'"

Before he'd even looked at the pages, Harry found himself defending the size of the role.

"There are no small parts," he said, quoting someone he'd heard on the Bravo channel, "only small actors."

He could tell that Megan didn't really buy that particular wisdom, but she had the good grace to be silent.

Harry looked at the pages and saw that "Hi" was indeed one of his lines; another was "Need some help?" But he was relieved to see that his third line had to do with Pushkin and seemed to be central to the plot. Harry had never actually read Pushkin, but he knew a lot *about* Pushkin. He felt he could really sink his teeth into the Pushkin line.

"Maybe when they see you, they'll think of another part you can do," said Megan.

Harry told her it didn't work that way.

"Besides," he said, testing her, "I'm not sure it's worth it to fly all the way back to Manhattan just to be an actor."

"Dad . . ." said Megan, going for the bait. "How can you say that? I looked at it again, and it's a *great* part. I'll even rehearse it with you.

"And I think I'll put some blonde streaks in for the premiere."

Before he got carried away and actually committed to the role, Harry thought he'd better run the proposal past Julie. She had given up her old job in carpentry and was now counseling troubled Hispanics in Manhattan. So she was unable to be in Miami with him. But she knew that Harry was going through a "rough patch" (her phrase, not Harry's). It had been a while since he had gotten a call from anybody to do anything.

"Your name," a Hollywood agent had told him, "no longer comes up on the radar screen."

Harry had begun, with less than amusement, to look at want ads for Security Guards. And since she loved Harry and always wanted the best for him, Julie had encouraged him to forget about the money and go to Miami to "refocus" or "regroup" or whatever he said he needed to do down there. ("Ramp up" was another one. He may have told her he needed to "ramp up.") And of course she wanted him to spend some time with their daughter.

Years back, when Harry had been having what he thought of as a casual, lightly-tethered affair with Vera Landers, he had met Julie behind a police barricade at a Gay and Lesbian parade in the West Village. And that was the end of that for Harry and other women – except for flirting, which he would never give up. Vera, it later dawned on him, had not been as casual as he thought about their affair – and had gone off to Hollywood at that point, possibly in a huff.

"I think you should do the part," said Julie, "but remember, she *is* after you."

"That's ridiculous," said Harry, who, after consideration, decided it wasn't that ridiculous. "Didn't I read somewhere that she had a kid with a guitar player?"

"I don't care how many kids she's had. She wants your bones. So watch yourself, big guy. And I love you."

"I love you, too."

Julie had taught him to say "I love you" at the end of all conversations, whether he felt like it or not. On automatic now, he had once said "I love you" to his accountant.

Harry was unable to reach Vera by phone, but he did get through to an assistant in Manhattan who said she was delighted – on Vera's behalf – that he had agreed to be in the movie. After taking Harry's measurements for Wardrobe, she gave him instructions on how to get to the set on the upper West Side. Since no mention was made of airline tickets or hotel accommodations, Harry concluded that he had been put in the category of people who were Friends of the Production and were just participating as a lark. And they were above such considerations as expenses and getting paid. Harry did not bring up any of this since he did not want to have to tell his daughter that he had blown the deal. He was still upset with himself for agreeing to send Megan away to boarding school. To compensate for that cold decision, he had virtually dedicated his life to supplying her with treats and making sure she had a trouble-free existence.

Harry arranged for an elderly Russian woman who was a year-round resident of the hotel to look in on Megan while he was away. His daughter had mentioned that a vanload of Lacrosse players from her school was going to be passing through Miami. He wanted to make sure she didn't hop on the van.

While he was packing, it occurred to Harry – and it bothered him – that he did not have time to lose enough weight to make a significant difference in his appearance. He did what he could by having Special K and skimmed milk for breakfast, drinking a lot of water, and eating only half the portion of stuffed veal that was served on the flight. It troubled him as well that there would be no time to do anything about his hair, which had whitened up in the Miami sun. He had a feeling that if he called the Manhattan salon and said "I have a little part in a movie," Dennis, though far from happy about it, would squeeze him in for a cut n'color on an emergency basis. But there wasn't enough time. And even if there had been, it would look as if he had come directly from the salon to the set. Harry's hair looked best when he was three days into a rinse. So he would just have to show up as a white-haired butterball.

Harry made his way through a small army of uniformly scruffy young people who were shouting into walkie-talkies. He gave his name to a woman in a tailored suit who appeared to be in authority. Barely looking up from her clipboard, she directed him to a holding area marked by a sign that said "Extras."

"Forgive me," said Harry, with the quiet confidence of a poker player holding a winning hand, "but I have a speaking role."

After checking a cast roster, the woman's attitude softened. She led him to a curbside trailer with a placard affixed to it marked "Daniel," the name of the character Harry was scheduled to play in the movie. Harry thanked the woman and made a mental note to thank Vera as well for the courtesy. He stepped inside the trailer and saw that his costume was neatly arranged on a bunk bed; the suit was not one Harry would have picked out for himself, but he tried it on all the same. It fit nicely, causing him to rethink his feelings about earth tones. The shoes, however, presented a problem. It was not just the tassels. Though Harry did not care much for tassels, he could understand that the character he played – who lived in a small town – might very well love them. But Harry had always been a tough fit when it came to shoes – he had a wide foot – and the tasseled shoes were particularly uncomfortable. He might have soldiered on with them, but he had a feeling that any discomfort he felt would creep into his performance. And no one would attribute it to the shoes. They would just conclude that he was a lousy actor. So he decided to wear his own shoes – which were as comfortable as bedroom slippers – and carry the tasseled ones to the set, just in case the cinematographer felt that Harry's shoes threw off the look of the picture.

Once Harry was fully costumed, the woman with the clipboard, who had been waiting in the street, led him off to a much larger trailer for hair and makeup. After briefly examining Harry's hair, the stylist decided that a snip here and there was all that was required; he made a big fuss over Harry's hair texture, calling over an assistant to share in his admiration for it.

Soon afterward, as Harry was having his makeup applied, a pretty young actress took a seat beside him. Chin in hand, she tucked her legs beneath her, as if she were about to listen to a lecture by her favorite professor. He recognized her as a star of Indie films. She said she had seen and admired one of Harry's Two Big Pictures on cable and wondered if he would have a drink with her sometime to discuss film.

"Absolutely," said Harry, who felt he could get such a meeting past Julie, considering its underlying serious nature.

The clipboard lady, who had become some kind of personal assistant, led Harry to the set itself – a huge loft that had been gotten up to look like a New England bookstore. Though Harry had the Two Big pictures and divided credits on a few adaptations, he had, surprisingly, never made an actual visit to a movie set. But he was on one now, in costume and carrying the tasseled shoes. Vera looked up from a trio of assistants and Harry thought – or imagined – he saw his and Vera's whole affair register on her face, like a split-second movie – straight through from his moth-eaten opening line ("You don't happen to be a model . . . ?") to her face-saving farewell salvo ("Just remember, Buddy, I'm the one who dumped *you*"). She didn't seem to have aged much – she still had the legs and the great hair – maybe a little hardness around the eyes and a slight stoop to her shoulders. She came toward him with a confident stride, extending a businesslike hand. Then, as if to say "the hell with it," she gave him a big hug and offered both her cheeks to be kissed. She glanced at Harry's shoes – and the tasseled ones he was carrying – and before he could explain she seemed to make a quick directorial decision and told him not to worry about a thing.

"You're going to be great," she said, with just the faintest tinge of a British accent. "And don't worry about the lines . . . so long as you don't drop any factual information."

"They're great lines," said Harry, one writer to another. "Why would I want to change them?"

Vera then introduced Harry to the male star. Though the actor had been described by the hair and makeup people as a wonderful human being, he did not come across as being all that wonderful to Harry.

"You do this often?" he asked Harry, after a perfunctory hand-shake and the hint of a sneer. Harry had only been sneered at once or twice in his life and he remembered each occasion.

"Only when I'm asked," said Harry, wondering what he had done to offend the man.

He then recalled that early in his career, the actor had been re-jected for a part in one of Harry's Two Big pictures. He had evi-dently held it against Harry, who – apart from putting in a good word for a girlfriend – had nothing to do with the casting. Harry noted with some surprise that the star seemed overweight and, frankly, quite slovenly, the type of fellow who bowls once a week for exercise. Considering the star's attitude toward him, Harry was somewhat gratified by this. Yet moments later, when it was time for the star to do a scene – and he had slipped into a smok-ing jacket and had his makeup freshened – he was transformed into the trim and handsome individual the movie-going public admired. Harry was aware of cinema magic, but this was ridiculous.

Harry was scheduled to play opposite the female star who

was generally cast as a pert and spunky – but not particularly sexy – type who was always challenging authority. As if to demonstrate a dimension of herself that had never been tapped, she was off in a corner of the set, doing hot Latino dance routines. Harry felt they came off as being stubbornly pert and spunky. Nonetheless, when Vera introduced Harry to the female star, he went into automatic flirt mode.

"My God," he said, "I'm standing here with America's sweetheart."

"I've heard about you," she said, acknowledging the flirt with a wagging finger.

When it was time for their scene, Vera called for quiet on the set. The response was immediate – a hushed and almost reverential silence. Harry wondered what might have happened if years back he had met *this* Vera, who commanded the respect and admiration of not only a huge cast and crew but of The Industry itself – instead of the disorganized teenager he had virtually found on 23rd Street on her way to a class at the Fashion Institute. Of course, *this* Vera might not have been terribly interested in Harry.

Vera showed Harry his "mark," assuring him once again that he was going to be fabulous. After sizing up the shot, she told Harry to go straight to his Pushkin line. Then she called for action. Harry had expected to begin with "Hi" and "Need any help?" The change in sequence threw him off stride. In addition, what suddenly seemed like the enormity of the moment began to get to him as well. There was so much at stake – a part in a major movie, the huge cast and crew looking on . . . all those careers . . . the millions being spent, even though he wasn't getting any . . . Though he had rehearsed the line on the plane, perhaps a bit too flamboyantly (the flight attendant had asked Harry if he was ill) his mind went blank. He was unable to bring forth a single word. Vera called for the cameras to stop rolling. She told Harry not to be upset.

"It happens all the time," she said.

After allowing Harry a moment to compose himself, she signaled for the action to begin again. On his second go-round, Harry got the words out.

"May I interest you in Pushkin?" he heard himself ask the female star. And then, taking a chance, he added the phrase, "Russia's greatest poet." Though he was not entirely pleased with his delivery, he saw Vera smile. With a little roll of her hand, she encouraged him to continue. Harry relaxed a bit then. Dipping into his knowledge of nineteenth-century Russia – and with the female star looking on, a tight smile on her face – Harry began to comment on the Tsar, the Winter Palace, the gorgeous imperial uniforms and Pushkin's financial problems. Gathering confidence, the bit firmly between his teeth, Harry gave a colorful account of Pushkin's fatal duel with his wife's paramour, raising the possibility that the poet's rival, D'Anthes, might have cheated by wearing a steel vest. He described in detail Pushkin's final moments and Nicholas II's graciousness in not only settling the poet's debts, but also establishing a trust fund for his family.

"Can you imagine an *American* President doing that for a poet?" was his rhetorical question to the stupefied actress.

"No, I can't," she ad-libbed flatly.

Then, as Harry paused, struggling to remember the names of Pushkin's survivors and the attending physician at the fatal duel, Vera signaled for the cameras to stop. She led the cast and crew in a round of applause.

"Was that a take or was that a take?" said Vera.

That led to a second round, that was even more enthusiastic.

Pulling Vera aside, Harry said : "I hope I didn't do too much."

"Oh, no," said Vera, "You did just enough."

Harry sailed through his brief remaining scene. With the Pushkin monologue in the bank, he saw no need to embellish his "Hi" and "Need some help?" dialogue. Feeling he was a genuine member of the cast now he was confident enough to ask the still photographer if she would mind taking a picture of him with the two lead actors. They agreed, the male star somewhat begrudgingly. But – always the star – he flashed a charming last-minute smile when the camera was actually pointed at him. That gave Harry a great souvenir for his daughter – and for his office wall, the main purpose of which was to impress repairmen. Not wishing to offend Vera, he asked for a picture to be taken with her as well, though he had a feeling it would not make it to the wall. With his arm draped across the director's shoulder, he felt unaccountably protective of her, which of course was absurd. Vera was a powerful force in the industry. Harry was hanging on by his thumbs. It crossed his mind that she might throw him a screenwriting bone. When he saw that no such offer would be forthcoming, he graciously thanked Vera for thinking of him as an actor and gave her a final hug. Then he waved an overhead goodbye to the cast and crew – like Nixon – and left the set.

Back in the trailer, Harry undressed, got into his own clothes, folded his costume neatly and placed it back on the bunk bed. He considered taking the tie – as another souvenir – but decided it would be tacky of him, even though he was convinced that people like Brad Pitt and Val Kilmer took home entire wardrobes and the studio didn't dare complain, for fear of alienating them on future projects.

And then Harry was back on the street . . . in the rain, no less – no hairdresser, no makeup artist, no stand-in (he'd actually had an extra with his measurements and a similar costume fill in for him during one of the breaks – presumably to save Harry's energy) – just another normal person at the end of the day. He felt sad about all this and realized he was experiencing a bittersweet moment. Even though Harry was pissed off at The Industry for turning its back on him, he had to concede that movies led the way when it came to bittersweet moments. Maybe the theatre too a little bit, but mostly the movies. When all else failed, you could always have some terrific actress (and now *Harry* was saying terrific) biting her lip (did Clinton get that from the movies?) or some actor suddenly realizing he'd made a romantic mistake and running through the rain so he could get back to the terrific actress before she was about to get on a plane and marry an accountant – and kiss her in the rain and everyone would forget they'd spent two hours being exposed to a stunted and moronic sensibility.

"How come they let you go on and on like that?" asked Megan, who had been examining her tan in the mirror.

"It wasn't my idea," said Harry, who had flown back to Miami and was in high spirits once again, the bittersweet moment just a memory. "I got my teeth into one of the lines, and the director told me to keep going."

"So you have a huge part now," said Megan.

"I wouldn't call it that. 'Substantial' is more like it."

"This means that we're definitely going to the premiere."

"Not necessarily," said Harry, who did not want to set up his daughter for a disappointment, although he himself had wondered if an invitation was part of his deal, such as it was. "The premiere is generally a benefit for rich people to raise money for a disease. But we'll definitely see the movie before the general public does."

"I hope so," said Megan, concentrating on the mirror. "And I don't understand why my legs get tan and my face is still white."

Harry awoke in the middle of the night with a horrible thought. He'd been sleeping lightly, playing back – and savoring – his Pushkin scene when it suddenly occurred to him that none of the cameras had been focused on him. Not that there weren't several in evidence. But they all seemed to be positioned behind Harry and trained on the female star – so that all of the shooting was over . . . and past . . . his shoulder. Harry calculated that during his Pushkin monologue, an audience would only be able to make out a sliver of his profile, if that. Harry was shaken and could not get back to sleep. He kept kicking himself for not being aware of the camera; if he had, he would have been able to crane his head around and get more of himself in. It took a great deal of self-discipline for him to prepare Megan's breakfast in the morning and not let on that something awful had happened. But later in the day, it occurred to Harry that perhaps there had been a camera that he had missed, a small discreetly placed one that was assigned to supporting players. And it had been trained on Harry. Or perhaps the main camera, through some technological advance – had the capability of curling around to pick up not only the female star's performance but Harry's as well. Only when Harry had considered these possibilities was he able to relax and to enjoy the rest of his stay in Miami.

Several months after returning to New York, Harry received an invitation for two to a screening of the movie for supporting players, hair and makeup people, cameramen, technical crew and various family members. Julie had graciously bowed out – the pressure of all her counseling. Megan had gotten a special pass from school so she could come down from Connecticut to attend the event along with Harry.

"What's a grip?" Megan wanted to know as they took the subway uptown to the screening.

"I'm not exactly sure," said Harry. "But grips, gaffers, they're behind-the-scenes people who work in the trenches and really make the movie happen."

"How come we have to go to the screening with them?" she asked

"It's not exactly a disgrace," said Harry, trying to be patient. "And you keep forgetting. I have a nice little part . . . but it's not as if I took over the whole production."

The movie, which fell under the heading of suspense/adventure, held Harry's attention for the first hour or so. But he could not tell if this was because it was good – or because he was in it. The story was multi-layered and the locales far-ranging. As he waited for his scenes to come up, Harry wondered how and where Vera, the kid he had virtually found on the street, had learned so much. She had never seemed the type to pore over Kurosawa films frame by frame. And yet here she was, entrusted with the fate of a big budget multi-tiered motion picture. As his admiration for her grew, Harry wondered – generally – what she would be like now as a lover. As he became older, his thoughts along that line became less specific. And then, out of loyalty to Julie, and a resistance to all the built-in complications, he put the whole business out of his mind.

"Are you enjoying it?" he asked Megan.

"Of course," said his daughter, who enjoyed most movies and was not discriminatory as to their content so long as they were made in the Nineties. "And quiet. Everyone can hear you."

Harry settled back in his seat, resigned to his fate, which was to spend a major part of what remained of his life trying to impress his fifteen-year-old daughter.

His first scene seemed to come out of nowhere. (Did they still call that a smash cut?) The action had been in a Brussels train station. Suddenly, there was Harry in a New England book store, greeting the leading lady. Much as he suspected, if not feared, there was very little of him to be seen, although he recognized his voice, which he'd been told, on occasion, was distinctive. Harry might have been disturbed by his fleeting appearance on the screen if he hadn't been so fascinated by the angle at which the camera had caught him. Harry was not shy about mirrors. Julie teased him about this – saying he was unable to pass one without a quick look – but this was an ambushing and extra-dimensional look at himself that he had never seen before – and that he imagined most people never get to see of themselves. The camera, predictably, was focused on the leading lady who was far more stunning than she had seemed to be in person; obviously the camera not only favored the actress, but was also head over heels in love with her. Harry – his character, that is – said "Hi" and asked if she needed any help and she said "Not just now." Then she strolled over to the Poetry Section, the camera lovingly following her while Harry disappeared from the frame.

"Did you see me?" Harry asked his daughter, lowering his voice this time.

"Sort of," said Megan. "But can I please watch the movie?"

With his Pushkin scene coming up shortly, Harry was able to damp down any general annoyance he felt and to settle back and enjoy whatever turned up on the screen. However, no sooner had the leading lady reached the Poetry Section than the action switched once again, this time to a furtive drug transfer on a dock in Cap Ferrat. And there was no Pushkin scene. Harry felt that a pail of ice water had been dumped on his neck, and at the same time – the contradiction notwithstanding – he would have sworn that smoke was coming out of his ears. To steady himself, he gripped both armrests, which resulted in an impatient look from Megan. Fainting was a possibility, canceled out only by Harry's fear of causing further embarrassment to his daughter. This is all ego, he told himself, stating the obvious. And what does it really mean in terms of a lifetime? In terms of the cosmos, for that matter? He had close friends who were writers, and had major credits on movies, much more important than Harry's. They had died recently and already been forgotten. Did anyone care if one of them had a role in a movie (which none of them had ever gotten, incidentally) – and a scene of theirs had been eliminated?

Gathering some stability, if not confidence, Harry reminded himself that the style of the film was to jump around in time. Maybe his Pushkin monologue had been folded into the climax where it might make some kind of ironic statement and have more impact. But when the picture ended with a series of brilliantly photographed explosions, Harry had to face the fact that his Pushkin scene had been eliminated. As he and Megan left their seats and crossed the lobby in silence, he felt that every eye was on him. His arthritic leg, which he'd always looked upon as an amusing inconvenience, ached so profoundly that he had to stop and sit for a minute opposite the refreshment stand.

For his ego, Harry passed up the subway and hailed a cab to take them home; and for Megan's sake, he kept what could only be called his humiliation in check. But as they approached the West Village, he could contain himself no longer.

"So what did you think?" he asked, bracing himself for her response.

"I thought you were great," she said. "And can we go to more screenings? I really enjoyed sitting with the grips."

Harry had been concerned about sending his daughter to school with all the spoiled and wealthy Connecticut Muffys and Buffys. Now he saw that in the crunch she was going to be all right. And that these were different times – and that maybe he had underestimated the Muffys and Buffys as well.

In the days that followed, Harry wondered if Vera had deliberately set out to punish him for the humiliation she'd felt when he had met and fallen in love with Julie – and begun to withdraw from Vera. (He hadn't done it suddenly – he had graciously taken both women to a New Year's Eve party.) But it was Julie who was surprisingly generous when Harry raised that possibility.

"Give her a break, Harry," she said. "She's got a lot more on her mind than embarrassing you. I'm sure you were good, but maybe the scene just didn't work in the movie."

And Harry realized that this was probably the case. The Pushkin scene, when he thought about it, was totally irrelevant. At one time, there had been a code named "Pushkin" but that had been dropped from the plot. So to let Harry do at least a ten-minute monologue on Pushkin – and to *include* it in the movie – just because he was good – would have been ridiculous. He even thought of calling Vera and telling her he understood why she had to make what was no doubt a painful decision – in case she thought he harbored some ill feeling. But whenever he tried to reach someone he knew in Hollywood, they were always in post-production ("So and So is in 'post'") and could not come to the phone, which made him feel even more sharply that he was left out of the party. So he did not make the call.

Harry's hurt feelings, like an old tennis injury, slowly began to disappear. The picture went into general release and Harry received a cassette from Vera's office. He'd been so upset at the screening that he had not even stayed for the credits. But he saw now that even though his part had been cut to a line – a line and a half to be generous – he was listed as "Daniel" when the credits rolled. Soon afterward, a golf bag arrived by Fed Ex, with the title of the film embroidered on the cloth. Even though Harry hated golf, he appreciated the touch. And he was delighted when a check for $500 came along in the mail with a note from the studio accountant saying he could keep it all – since the law permitted an individual to make one picture without joining and paying dues to the Screen Actor's Guild. And though the check did not quite cover Harry's airline tickets and traveling expenses, he appreciated the courtesy. And didn't actors get residuals? Once the movie turned up on television, other five hundreds might be coming along as well.

And then Harry started to get the calls. The first came from Julie's sister, Patsy, who had seen the film in a little theatre, just down the road from her Rape Crisis Intervention Center in the deep South. She thought Harry was excellent. And then Lenny, his old college roommate, called from Nebraska. A sports announcer now in Omaha, Lenny's great disappointment in life was that he had never cracked the networks.

"At first I heard the voice," he said, in the dramatic announcing style that had failed to impress CBS, "and then, to my great surprise, there was my old buddy on the big screen. I've been telling everybody for years that you were going to make it, and I was right. I'm proud of you, Harry, and I'm sure that all of Omaha feels the same way I do."

Half a dozen more calls followed, including one from Megan who said she had taken a group of girls from her dorm to see the movie. Not only had they enjoyed it, but they loved Harry's acting as well. And then Harry received what he considered the ultimate compliment. He was eating alone one night in an Italian restaurant on Thompson street – which was not unusual. Julie was so wasted during the week from her counseling that she pretty much collapsed when she got home on weekdays. It was all she could do to watch an episode of *Will And Grace*. Harry was about to dig into his main course when an attractive man he recognized as having appeared in several episodes of the *The Sopranos* approached his table and said he'd seen Harry in the movie.

"I thought you did an excellent job."

"But I went by in a flash," said Harry.

"Never mind," said the fellow, his voice taking on an ominous tone that Harry recognized from the hit series. "What I liked is that you didn't try to do too much. You kept it neat. You were very professional."

Harry could not have been more pleased. Along with so many Americans, Harry had been captivated by the television phenomenon. Julie had even worked the advisory "Don't call during the *Sopranos*" into her answering machine message which delighted many of their friends. The actor who stopped at Harry's table was not a regular – he'd had bit parts in two or three episodes – but to receive a compliment from anyone who had anything to *do* with the series was high praise indeed. It occurred to Harry that maybe he had been on screen a little longer than he realized – and that more of his face was recognizable than he had previously thought. He'd been so upset that he had probably never sat back and taken in the full impact of what he now thought of as his performance.

And so what began as a disaster for Harry turned out to have a surprisingly bright side. This was not an unusual development in his life. One of Harry's casual interests was military history. A favorite episode came about in the Franco-Prussian War, when all seemed lost for the Gallic nation; and then, all of a sudden, and out of nowhere, Ricciotti Garibaldi, the foreign recruit, rose up in the Cote D'Or; with his ragtag army of *francs-tireurs*, he began to cut through the German lines and to show that France still had teeth. France lost the war, and for that matter, Harry might lose his war as well. But that was beside the point. Whenever Harry was down on his luck there always seemed to be a Garibaldi in his life. Acting was his new Garibaldi.

Not that he took it seriously. He had never even taken *screenwriting* seriously and he had done it most of his life. But just for fun, Harry began to calculate the kinds of roles he could play. Not the kind where he'd actually have to act. He wasn't about to sign up for lessons at The Actors' Studio. But the kind where he could just more or less show up and be himself. He could do writers, of course, and people in related professions, such as William Morris agents. He couldn't do Mexican bandits, but he could certainly do judges. He felt confident – with his hair – that he could play the hell out of judges. So if he could get a judge part here and there and maybe a role as a teacher – he had actually taught screenwriting at a community college for a couple of weeks up in Vancouver – if he could land a few judge and teacher parts here and there and pick up some more of those five hundreds and string it all together he'd have a nice little income to go with his pension. Throw in Julie's counseling money and maybe they could stick·it out after all in financially strangulating Manhattan and not have to move to Flushing.

One thing he would not do, however, is audition. He'd move to Flushing – and the hell with what everybody thought – before he'd do that. That's all he would need is to be standing around with a bunch of old guys, skilled old guys with real acting track records, guys who did Falstaff with the *Lunts* for Christ's sakes, waiting around to try out for a judge part or a doorman. And that's probably what they'd want him to audition for, too, a doorman role, one who was about to retire with a heart condition and all the tenants come by to tell him how much they're going to miss him.

Let's say a Judge part did come up – or the hell with it, let's say it was a doorman role after all, just for argument's sake. . . . He might *read* – just go down there and read a few lines – so that they could get a feel for his capabilities and what he would be like in the role – but only – and he was firm about this – only if he knew the director – or at least *someone* in the production. It wasn't that he needed the fix to be put in. It wasn't that at all. He just wanted to know that he wasn't wasting his time, that he didn't go all the way down there for nothing . . . that he had a pretty damned good shot at getting the part. Otherwise, if it couldn't be set up that way, if they wouldn't allow him to just read informally, with no commitment on anyone's part, theirs, or *Harry's* for that matter, if they couldn't do that much for him, then forget it. . . . They could keep the fucking part and get somebody else to do it.

Some poor bastard who really needed the work.

Protect Yourself At All Times

THERE WAS NO EVIDENCE that it was a grudge match. To the contrary, the fighters touched gloves respectfully at the end of each brutal round. Yet few in the arena could recall seeing two men in a boxing ring attack each other with such savagery. One was a pale square-shouldered Irish middleweight with a conventional straight-ahead style, the other a Jamaican who was listed at the same weight but was much scrawnier than his opponent. He had, nonetheless, what the boxing analysts call a "wide repertoire" of skills. Both men had decent but not especially distinguished records in the ring. There was nothing in their previous matches to indicate they were capable of fighting at such a high level and with such unrelieved intensity. Yet something in each man seemed to tap into a well of fury in the other. They did not bother to feel each other out. At the opening bell, they flew at one another and began to trade punches to the head and body – a furious exchange that had the crowd in a state of frenzy. Before the third round had ended, the excited television announcers were already calling it The Fight of the Year.

Philip Collins, a retired high school teacher, watched the action on a television set in a small apartment above a Greek restaurant in the Chelsea district of Manhattan. He was a tall, slender man who was, at 73, a bit stooped over. Though his hair had turned white, he had lost little of it. And he still had the strong profile that had led more than one person to ask if he was a film actor.

Collins had intended to thaw out his frozen dinner in the microwave, but the televised fight was so riveting that he did not want to get up from his recliner and miss a moment of it. He had followed the sport for many decades. When he was a boy of five, Collins' father, who had a milk delivery route in the East Bronx, had taken him to see his first fight – one that was held in an outdoor arena. Collins became a fan of a local heavyweight named Tami Mauriello who fought in the main event that night. Later in his career, he gained recognition with a knockdown of the great Joe Louis in the first round of their championship fight. The astonished Louis had recovered and finished off Mauriello before the round ended. Whenever Collins discussed the fight, he was quick to point out that one of Mauriello's legs was shorter than the other, so that he could only move in a forward direction. The predictable style unfortunately made him easy prey for a skilled opponent.

Collins himself had never done any boxing and only once had he been tempted to enter the ring. He had signed up to participate in an amateur fight sponsored by The Police Athletic League. But the night before the fight, he was so sick with worry about what might happen to him that he was unable to sleep. In the morning he threw up and his mother had to call ahead on his behalf and cancel.

The memory of what he thought of as an act of cowardice stayed with him for years. Nonetheless, he continued to follow the major fights on the radio. So vivid was the announcing style of Don Dunphy that Collins felt he was actually in the arena for the event being broadcast. He was able to visualize every punch thrown, each knockdown. He learned the meaning of certain code words. For example, when a fighter was described as being "game," Collins knew that he was on his way to defeat.

As a GI, during the Korean War, Collins became ill one day and ran a fever of one hundred and four. Yet he managed virtually to crawl out of a hospital bed in San Diego and make it to an enlisted men's club in time to watch Rocky Marciano knock out "Jersey Joe" Walcott in the first round of their televised championship rematch. He had his favorites, Ali, of course, and Henry Armstrong, and a middleweight few remembered named Johnny

Bratton. The Chicago fighter had seal black shoulder-length hair that bounced each time he hit or got hit. He was not much of a puncher, but he had a style that was clean and pure, more so than any boxer Collins had ever seen. Collins loved to *talk* fights, at saloons, or on social occasions when he ran into another enthusiast. He would always steer the conversation around to the "phantom punch" Ali used to defeat Sonny Liston in their Lewiston, Maine rematch. ("I've watched that tape a dozen times and I still haven't seen the punch.") He made sure to mention that he was actually there at the Garden for the first Ali-Frazier fight. In the same arena, he had seen Roberto Duran, an unknown teenager from the back streets of Panama, literally spit at the then champion Ken Buchanan of Scotland before knocking him out in the thirteenth round. To Collins, the very names of past fighters were like poetry . . . Charles "Bobo" Olson, Kid Gavilan, Harry Greb, Benny Leonard and the southpaw Lou Tendler. Al "Bummy" Davis, Tony Canzoneri and Arturo Godoy. Kid Chocolate, Pipino Cuevas and Willie Pastrano. Though he admired Evander Holyfield, he winced each time the heavyweight was introduced as Evander "The Real Deal" Holyfield. Was this a plea for his authenticity? Collins had always felt the nickname struck a wrong note.

Collins had lost his wife in a car accident. In the years following her death, he had met and enjoyed the company of several women. But such was the depth of his love for his wife that he had never once thought of remarrying. He raised their one child alone. They lived in a small house on Long Island; from time to time, Colleen would join her father in the den and watch the fights with him. Now and then he made stray comments about the sport. "When you have a guy hurt, step back and let him fall. Keep punching and you're liable to revive him."

In fighting a south paw, he instructed his daughter, the trick was to circle to the left of his front foot.

"That takes away his left hook. . . . And always throw punches in combinations. You don't throw one and then step back to admire your handiwork. That leaves you vulnerable to a counterpunch."

On occasion, as Collins watched a fight, he would unconsciously duck punches, cover up his ribs and throw a punch when he saw an opening.

"Dad, you're not in the ring," she would remind him.

When a fight turned vicious – or more than most – he would say to her "Maybe you shouldn't watch this."

"It's all right," she would assure him. "I enjoy it."

He did not try too hard to dissuade her. It was comforting for Collins to have her beside him in what he had come to think of – since his wife's death – as an empty house.

But now and then he asked himself: What am I doing? Why am I letting her watch two men try to pound each other into oblivion? He tried to justify this by telling himself – and her – that it was a sport. The best fighters were great athletes, their movements balletic. They rarely got hurt. But he could not think of too many examples to prove his point. Ali himself had had at least five fights too many. No one could claim that he had walked away from the sport uninjured. So there was a part of Collins that felt awful about exposing his daughter to such carnage, especially since many of the televised fights were one-sided. Managers served up bloated, over-the-hill "tomato cans" to fatten up the records of rising stars. At a cocktail party, Collins had once met a psychiatrist, a father and presumably a learned man, who was also a boxing fan and, as a hobby, had actually managed several fighters.

"How do we justify our interest in this bloody sport?" he'd asked the man. "Two men trying to destroy each other?"

The man, who seemed not to have a worry in the world, had shrugged and said" "We don't."

His response was of interest to Collins, but it was not terribly helpful.

Collins had constructed a scenario in which his daughter would always be with him. She would travel with him to China, a dream of his – and she would look after him when he was unable to take care of himself. (He had never considered the unfairness of such an arrangement.) As it happened, Colleen enrolled in a junior college nearby where she met and fell in love with the first boy she had dated seriously. They married, and before they'd graduated, moved to La Jolla so that they could be near the young man's family. Rather than remain alone in an isolated area, Collins, in his sixties, sold the house and moved back to New York City where he had been born. Though Manhattan offered a feast of activity, Collins took advantage of very little of it. He'd once enjoyed the theatre but the ticket prices seemed annoyingly high, and it became increasingly difficult for him to hear the stage dialogue. So he stopped going to see plays. His few friends died. He kept in touch with his daughter, but neither had much of a phone style. They ended each conversation by saying "I love you." But the exchanges were brief and strained. Perhaps he felt she had deserted him.

Though Collins' life had begun to narrow down, his interest in the fights never wavered. He saw one boxing program at an arena on Staten Island and had been surprised – and frightened – by the unruliness of the crowd. His age no doubt contributed to a feeling of vulnerability. But he recalled the fight nights of his youth as being convivial affairs. Men dressed for such occasions. They greeted each other warmly and exchanged cigars. There were catcalls but they were in a different spirit, jocular, never obscene. To throw refuse into the ring because of a disputed decision was unthinkable. It was a gentleman's sport. Or such was his recollection.

Collins was content now to kick back in his recliner and watch the fights at home on a television screen. More programs than ever were available on the cable channels. Once in a while he caught a gem, such as the unheralded bout between the powerful Irishman and the rangy and skillful Jamaican. Halfway along in the brutal ten-round fight match, there was an expectation that the fight would taper off. It was impossible for the fighters to continue at that level. But if anything, the action intensified. As if by silent agreement, the fighters took turns battering each other. The Irish fighter threw body punches with such force it seemed the Jamaican would be cut in two. And then, seemingly at the point of collapse, the slender Jamaican would find enough energy and willpower to fire back with a blizzard of slicing punches to the head that were thrown with speed that was impossible to follow. This was the pattern for ten furious rounds, Collins winced when the Irish fighter threw body blows, and covered up as if to block the scissor-like combinations of the Jamaican. Though the fighters were relatively unknown, the announcers, who were hoarse with excitement, made comparisons to the legendary fights of the past . . . Sadler/Pep . . . Leonard/Hearns . . . the Ali/Frazier fights . . . Zale/Graziano . . . When the bell sounded at the end of the tenth and final round, the referee raised the hands of both exhausted fighters. The fight was declared a draw. The crowd roared its approval.

There were two other tenants on the second floor of Collins' brownstone. One was a stout and cheerful nurse in her fifties, the other a retired 70-year-old City Hall worker, who favored checkered suits and wore a fedora at a rakish angle. Three days after the fight, Miss Simms, the nurse, passed Collins' door and heard the sound of a daytime soap opera on the television. She had not seen him at the corner coffee shop for several days, which was unusual. It was possible he'd gone somewhere and forgotten to turn off the set, but she had never known him to do any traveling. He liked his privacy – she was aware of that – but something prompted her to ring his doorbell to say hello and see how he was getting along. When there was no response, she became uneasy. At the newsstand, she ran into Mr. Adler, the jaunty City hall retiree. After exchanging pleasantries, she expressed her concern to him.

"Come to think of it," he said, "I haven't seen him around either."

The two decided to notify Antoine, the bartender at the Greek restaurant, who had a passkey to each of the brownstone apartments. All three mounted the stairs to the second floor. Antoine rang the bell several times, then rapped at the door. When no one came to answer, he used the passkey. The door swung open and there was Collins in his recliner, hunched over in a fighter's crouch. His nose was flattened, his lips puffed up, his ears battered and misshapen. There were mounds of swollen flesh around his eyes, which had become little slits, giving him a simian look.

"Oh, my God," said a horrified Miss Sims.

"We'd better call 9-1-1," said Antoine.

Mr. Adler removed his hat.

"Poor bastard," he said. "I hope he gave as good as he got."

Three Balconies

AS IS THE CASE with most men, Harry wanted to be taken seriously and resented the suggestion that he was not a serious man. Yet there may have been some truth to the charge. Because if he were to take a hard look at his life – which is not something he did every twenty minutes – he would have to admit that he had spent most of it chasing women. Or maybe not exactly chasing them, but pursuing them. Something along those lines. Which is not to suggest that he had a sterling record of catching them – or even knew what to do with them when he did – but he certainly did pursue them. Harry was still at it, but what bothered him was that he had done so much of it when he should have been reading Herodotus. He was reading Herodotus now, but if he had been reading Herodotus when he was chasing – or pursuing – women, he could have been finished with Herodotus and moved on to someone like Tacitus. Or Willa Cather. He could have been finished with Willa Cather, too, instead of just starting to read her.

Harry had once sat on the deck of a film producer's house in Malibu, exchanging stories about the carefree '60s and '70s. With a casual wave, the producer said that he had slept with hundreds of women.

"And I took no prisoners," he said, with grim satisfaction. Harry was not in that league. He had taken plenty of prisoners. And he did not want to get into a numbers game with the producer. He knew for a fact that the man had slept with entire platoons of film stars. Or at least he didn't doubt it. (The producer had a kind of sleazy charm. Harry could see him sleazing film stars into bed.) And Harry was painfully aware that in all his years of traveling to the Coast he had slept with only one film star, who, strictly speaking, wasn't really a film star at all but a catalog model who had left the business after playing a role in one movie. When Harry last heard from her, she was selling real estate in Sydney, or some-place like that.

But one thing Harry knew for sure was that he had at least chased – or pursued – women with the best of them.

Did that make Harry a womanizer? Did they still have wom-anizers in the '90s? And wasn't that someone who preyed on women and got them to sign over real estate holdings?

If so, that didn't sound much like Harry.

There were probably one or two women out there who would say that he had ended an affair too abruptly – or had pretended to be interested in them when all he wanted to do was roll around a little – but that would be the extent of his womanizing.

So if someone insisted that Harry was a womanizer, he would say fine, you got it, but would you please put an asterisk in there somewhere?

Harry was madly in love with his wife (he never failed to in-sert "madly" when he told someone how much he loved Julie), but he kept chasing women anyway. Yet never in the fifteen years they had been married had Harry had a full-out affair. (Or "conducted" one. He was fascinated by the image of someone "conducting" an affair.) Harry was scared out of his wits at the very thought of having an affair. The last thing he needed was to lose Julie. He had come close to having an affair on two – maybe two and a half – occasions (over-flirted is the way he saw it) and all of a sudden it was hey-wait-a-minute-this-is-the-big-leagues-what-do-I-do-now? What he had done was to take himself – physically – out of the country. He had gone off to play blackjack in the Caribbean – Harry's equivalent of a cold shower. It was fair to say that he had gambled his way out of the two and a half affairs.

You just didn't have affairs when you were married to some-one like Julie. To actually enter another woman – and then go back and sleep with Julie. A little unthinkable is what it was.

But that did not stop Harry from charging out of the gate every chance he got to see how he would do out there. On an impulse, Harry had fired a famous agent, in a sense shooting himself in the foot, since the assignments had dried up overnight. (And he could feel the agent's fine hand in drying them up.) When he tried to hire another (less-famous) agent, the fellow had said: "Harry, I am afraid your name no longer comes up on the radar screen."

That fact notwithstanding, he and Julie got by. He did a little of this and a little of that and actually made some money in real estate, which embarrassed him slightly – as if it made him a less serious man. One of the small jobs Harry got offered was to write about hobbies for what he thought of as an "old guy" quarterly. Harry struggled with the assignment for a few weeks until he realized that his only hobby was chasing women. And obviously what the fellows at the "old guy" quarterly had in mind was lacquering or sanding stuff in the garage. Collecting sheriffs' badges – something like that. So that was the end of the assignment.

When Harry was younger, he chased women – or went after them, or whatever he did – because they looked and smelled and felt nice and he wanted to go to bed with them. (Not "bed" them. There was a certain type of individual who "bedded" women and Harry was not one of them.) But now Harry enjoyed listening to women and finding out what they did and what was on their minds instead of just waiting for them to finish talking so he could shift into his seduction mode.

Was it possible he just liked to be with women? One of his favorite things was when he met someone he had at one time thought of as a "pretty young thing," somebody's assistant, and have her turn out to be a leading neurophysiologist. Or a feared litigator. It seemed that half the women he ran into were feared litigators. He was now surprised when one of them turned out *not* to be a feared litigator. And Harry was delighted by this change in the culture. How could he not be? In his lifetime – as a phenomenon – he ranked it up there with the overnight collapse of communism.

That thought – and the others – occurred to Harry as he sat on the eighteenth-story balcony of a hotel suite in Miami Beach and considered ending his life with a little hop over the four-foot brass railing. Several years before, he had crushed three toes in an ancient garage door – they looked like cartoon toes, he had told friends – and he could not imagine it would be more painful to hit the pavement. Additionally, and in support of his impulse, he had heard that you would lose consciousness while in flight. Of course, no one knew if you woke up for a split second before you landed – and what that would be like. In any case, Julie would be all right. She would have the embarrassing money from Harry's real estate deals and the royalties that still dribbled in from his Two Big Pictures. And she would have little difficulty finding a new friend. All she had to do was decide she wanted one. Julie kept her weapons concealed, but when she decided to zero in – and Harry had seen her in action – you (i.e. the target) were a dead duck. Megan would get along fine as well. She was an independent thing at thirteen, and she had shocked Harry by announcing that she wanted to go to a boarding school. So how much did she need Harry around?

If Harry took that little hop over the brass railing – and he was amazed at how easy it would be – he would not have to go around feeling so awful.

It was the day following Harry's third night of chasing women and drinking more than he wanted to, and he could not recall a time when he had been shakier. And this was without drugs and cigars. If you had thrown that pair into the mix, he would have been over the railing hours before.

As was his custom, Harry had flown to Miami a week in advance of his wife and daughter – this time to check on the condo they had bought, which was under construction, and, as always, to see if he could get some work done in a fresh setting. The director of a small theatre in Los Angeles had expressed interest in Harry's new Siege of Malta play but felt it lacked a romantic component. His suggestion was that Harry thread a Diane Sawyer type through the play – someone covering the siege for some medieval publication, or maybe a broadside – and have her fall in love with one of the Knights Templar; he didn't care which one. Ostensibly, that is why Harry had flown to Miami a week in advance of his family. If he could pull it off – successfully thread a Diane Sawyer type through the play – he would have a production on Melrose Avenue, right under the noses of the studio executives and agents who said he was off the radar screen. A hit, of course, would put Harry right back on the screen.

But so far, Harry had not even taken the play out of the Sports Sac, much less begun to thread through a Diane Sawyer type – which is one of the reasons he felt so awful. He had warmed up for the Miami trip at home on Long Island – taken a kind of trial run – at a local bar, and he recalled closing out the evening by telling a mortgage broker that there was "something about her," a kind of "sly beauty" that other people might not notice but that Harry noticed and found irresistible. Yes, he was a little married – he never lied about such things – but he had to have her. If he was not mistaken – and he hoped he was – he had also told her that as an artist, he did not "play by other people's rules." (Obviously, that was the kind of dialogue that had gotten him removed from the radar screen.) So he probably had said that, and all the other things as well, and he had meant them at the time. It was a good thing he hadn't invited her to fly down to Miami with him, which he was capable of doing at the time. Because that's all he would have needed – to wind up not playing by other people's rules with a mortgage broker in Miami Beach. And with his family on their way down.

But somehow Harry had gotten up the next morning and made it to the airport – and once he had landed and rented the Mitsubishi Galant, he started to revive; when he saw the sign on I-95 that said WELCOME TO MIAMI BEACH and the comforting one nearby – MT. SINAI MEDICAL CENTER – he revived with a vengeance.

By the time Harry pulled up to the hotel, he was so excited about the weather and how balmy it was and how good he felt that he didn't even bother to unpack. He took a shower, dressed, slapped on some of the new uni-sex cologne, put a salsa recording on full blast in the Galant (one that had been highly recommended by a hot little trotter behind the Alamo counter) and tore into the beach like a madman.

Harry's plan was to work his way up and down the beach, making a few of the night people he knew from the previous year aware that he was back. But as it turned out, he never made it past his first stop. It was a small hotel, a few blocks from the ocean, one that Harry remembered as having a cheerful feeling to it and a little bar he thought of as an excellent place to get started. But something had changed since his last visit. It still had the cheerful feeling, but it had caught fire and turned into a madhouse; it was jammed with tanned and pretty and handsomely turned-out women who Harry correctly identified as young Miami Beach professionals. Each wore an outfit that you didn't just throw on. The outfits took a lot of planning and it was clear that these women took Saturday night seriously. Harry, on the other hand, had forgotten how important it was. In Manhattan, Saturday night was referred to by knowledgeable bar people as "amateur time."

The mood was tastefully raucous, and the activity spilled out from the bar into the lobby and out to a packed terrace ringed with lanterns, giving it some kind of enchanted look. Or at least Harry thought so.

There was no question that Harry was the oldest one in the place, and he was sorry he hadn't lost a few pounds and picked up a quick suntan before the flight. But what really bothered him was that his hair wasn't right. In preparation for the trip, he had had it colored or rinsed – rinsed was the term he preferred. But the colorist, or rinser (who had once done Julie's hair) had made a remark about Julie's hairstyle that was just a fraction off and

Harry, still wearing his apron, had marched out of the salon in the middle of the rinse. (Criticize Harry to your heart's content, but be careful what you say about Julie.) Whatever the case, there was some question as to whether Harry's rinse had taken. It may have been a little patchy, and someone with a discerning eye – some young Miami Beach professional who had started out as a beautician – would probably notice that he'd had an incomplete rinse. But Harry's position was that the subdued lights, especially the enchanted ones on the terrace, would disguise the possible unevenness of his rinse. And if he managed to fake out only half the women in the crowd, that was fine with him.

And he would make up for the rinse and the weight and the age – don't forget that – by the sheer force of his joy at being with this new group of tanned and attractive young Miami Beach professionals on a Saturday night, the importance of which he had forgotten but which they took seriously.

So Harry ordered a double scotch and waded into the crowd.

He met women quickly and easily and what amazed him was how relaxed his swing was – he didn't even have to shoehorn his credits into the conversation. And that was just as well because his Two Big Pictures had been made twenty years before and he was starting to get vague looks when he mentioned them. But all he had to do on this particular Saturday night in Miami Beach was to say Hi, how are you doing? And isn't it great to be here? And if someone suggested it was a little crowded, Harry would say he didn't mind, since he lived reclusively most of the year. He found himself saying that a lot – that he lived reclusively – so he must have liked the sound of it.

No sooner did Harry get started speaking to one woman than he went spinning – or got spun off – to another, which was fine with him. Not surprisingly, he met a few litigators. But he also spoke to a woman who designed halo braces for people who broke their necks in highway accidents. Her father, who had wanted her to take over his luggage business, had broken his neck in a highway accident and she had gotten to design a halo brace for him – which Harry and the woman agreed was quite a story. So Harry had spent a bit more time with her than what he had in mind. And then a tiny woman in black leather asked if Harry could help her get a drink. And Harry, only too happy to oblige, had lifted her off the floor so the bartender could see her. She turned out to be the manager of a Chicago rock group, and after she had gotten her drink, she said she'd like to get to know Harry, though she was tied up with the band on that particular night. That was fine with Harry. He turned his attention to a pretty young student who was getting a degree in business, though, frankly, all she wanted to do was lie on the beach and do nothing – which Harry found charming. He found everything charming and continued to do so for two days running, returning to the same spot on Sunday night and finding it only a little more subdued. Throughout this mild escapade, he kept noticing a couple – in the same two seats at the bar – who had been taking in the scene and at the same time having a whispered conversation. The woman, who appeared to be in her mid-twenties, had tanned shoulders and streaky blonde hair that was cut short in a style Harry recognized from one of Julie's fashion magazines. She wore a white lingerie-type halter that did not cover her breasts so much as present them. As to the breasts themselves, they may not have been perfect – what are perfect breasts? – but they were close enough to the mark for Harry. He assumed she was a fashion model – what else could she be? – and that her companion, a thin fellow with a thin face, was somehow tied to the fashion industry.

She was the most exquisite creature he had ever seen and Harry knew immediately that she was out of his league. Strictly speaking, she should have been out of the thin fellow's league, too, but she wasn't – that's the way life is.

Then, amazingly, because that's the kind of three days it had been, Harry was talking to her. For all he knew – in the crush of activity – she may have turned and begun speaking to him. Harry loved surprises and got a big one when it turned out she wasn't a model at all – she was Miriam Rosen, a Jewish, or half-Jewish, housewife with two children, from Guatemala of all places. No disrespect to Guatemala – which to its credit had just ended a thirty-year war with its guerrillas – but Harry had no idea they had Miriam Rosens running around down there. Ones who were this gorgeous. So obviously, Harry would have to rethink his feelings about Guatemala. The thin fellow with the thin face did not seem to mind Harry talking to Miriam Rosen – he even encouraged it with a careless wave of his hand, as if to say, Please continue, this means nothing to me. So Harry continued talking to Miriam Rosen and – like a beginning swimmer – found it easier as he went along. The couple were mysterious about what they were to each other, and Miriam encouraged Harry to take a guess: Were they friends? Husband and wife? Lovers? Like a contestant in a game show, Harry chose lovers. Then, after pointing out that he was a story-teller (who lived reclusively most of the year) he fashioned a scenario in which Miriam Rosen was a married woman who had gone off to meet the thin man, her lover, for a weekend idyll; on Monday, after several days of exquisite lovemaking, she would fly back to her family in Guatemala, refreshed, happy, better able to be a housewife and mother. (He did not speculate on the future of her lover.)

As Harry told the story, he was aware that it wasn't much. Even if he were back on the radar screen, he would never have pitched it to a studio.

The banality of the story notwithstanding, Miriam Rosen was delighted with it, wriggling around in her seat and clapping her hands and indicating that Harry had absolutely nailed the situation.

"You are very wise," said the thin man with the thin face, stroking his chin as if he were a little wise himself and what you had here was an exchange between two wise individuals.

Harry was impressed by how nicely they were all getting along; the thought crossed his mind that the three of them might even end up in the couple's hotel suite, with the thin-faced man graciously allowing Harry to make love to Miriam Rosen while he went off to an adjoining room to stare at the ocean and smoke a Gauloise.

After all, if the couple liked Harry's first story, why wouldn't they like this one, which, in Harry's view, had a lot more dimension?

Then Miriam Rosen said, "I've been watching you for two nights now and I think you're very courageous."

"Because I'm old?" said Harry.

"No, no, no," said Miriam Rosen, but the two extra no's were confirmation that he had read her correctly – and that tore it for Harry.

He hung around for a while and then said he had to get going, but that if he ever found himself in Guatemala, he would be sure to look up Miriam Rosen. Then he made as graceful an exit as was possible under the circumstances, paying his check and giving a little farewell salute to the bartender. Amazingly, he found the Galant in the public parking lot with little difficulty; then he took a long drive with no particular destination in mind and found himself way out on the Tamiami Trail at four in the morning. He stopped at a topless nightclub, which was empty except for three men in shirt sleeves who were arguing at the bar and ignoring the one dancer who was still working. She had long black hair and good legs, but her jawline was a little off and she did some sudden and erratic moves around a tent pole that Harry found unsettling. When she finished her routine, she approached Harry – who was tapering off with a Molson – and said the place was about to close, but if he was interested, she might be able to squeeze in one last private lap dance. Harry was probably the only one in America who didn't know the specifics of lap dances, but he felt he needed to get something out of the three nights, so he said fine and followed her to a darkened booth at the rear of the club. She told him to keep one eye out for her boss, which he did, though it wasn't very relaxing. Then she did the lap dance for Harry, who was surprised at how intimate that type of dance could be. Or maybe they were that way only at closing time in this particular club. Maybe they even called it a "closer." Before he knew what had happened to him, he was unbuckled and she had swooped down on him with a couple of her sudden, erratic tent pole moves. And then he was back in the Galant, asking himself what kind of serious man allows himself to get lap danced on the Tamiani Trail by a dancer whose jawline is a little off. When he could have been back at the hotel reading Herodotus.

He was still asking himself that question the next day as he sat on the balcony of his hotel suite thinking that maybe he ought to hop over the railing and bring down the curtain once and for all. There was a fellow who had done just that from a similar balcony two floors above. He had run up debts all over the beach, and the police had come for him and put him in handcuffs; but they had forgotten about his feet, and he was able to break away and make it over the railing. When Harry told Julie about it, she asked: "What happened to him?" That was one of the thousand things he loved about her. She could hear a story like that and think something good had come of it.

Harry would never go over the railing because of debt. He didn't love debt, but there was no point to ending your life because of it. Declare bankruptcy in Florida and you're a hero. They practically run a benefit for you.

But Harry would do it because of being sixty and walking around with half a rinse and chasing women and not catching them and pissing away three whole days in which he hadn't even taken his Siege of Malta play out of the Sports Sac, much less begun to thread a Diane Sawyer type through it. (Which, incidentally, was the dumbest idea he had ever heard, even if it meant the play would get done in L.A. and give him a shot at getting back on the radar screen.)

So Harry clutched the sides of the beach chair, thinking it would anchor him down, which was ridiculous, since it was made of lightweight plastic. And he did not particularly relish the idea of being the first fellow to fly off a balcony holding on to a plastic chair.

But he could not drive the possibility out of his mind. He even did a dry run in which he imagined himself going over. He actually tried out a little whinnying sound he would make in the process, or maybe *whimpering* was closer to it – a salute to T.S. Eliot, demonstrating that in his final moment, Harry had not lost touch entirely with his literary concerns.

Sitting out on the balcony, gripping the arms of the plastic beach chair, Harry tried to push his thoughts in another direction. He had brought a couple of Willa Cather paperbacks out on the ledge with him (suddenly it was a ledge, not a balcony). He tried a few pages of one, but the descriptions of the bleak Nebraska plains – and the unforgiving land – were so desolate they made him feel even worse. So he set the book aside, thinking he had chosen the wrong Cather. Or maybe it was the right Cather, but he had tried it at an inappropriate time. Still, the very thought that there might be a more appropriate time was useful.

So Willa Cather had helped him out after all, even though, strictly speaking, he had not really plunged into her work.

The trick, Harry realized, was to get off the balcony and back into the hotel suite. Instead of sitting out there and arm-wrestling with himself. Or arm-wrestling with the *fates* – that was better. Obviously, he did not do well on balconies. So why sit out on them and try to become brilliant at it.

The trick was to get back into the hotel suite and get the place neatened up for Julie and Megan. And then take a walk, a simple solution that had always helped. And when he felt better, after the walk, at least take the Siege of Malta play out of the Sports Sac. Or maybe even leave it in the Sports Sac and start something entirely new. Trust his unconscious for a change, the way he did when he was writing his Two Big Pictures. See if it would lead him in a fresh direction – toward something like The War of Jenkins' Ear, which the L.A. producer might like even more than the Siege of Malta. The title alone would probably attract DeNiro.

And then try to stay in for at least one night. Watch a biography on Jefferson, someone like that. One that finally brought the man into focus, so you didn't have to keep hearing about his complexities. And if he had to go out, try to find a place that was a little more seasoned, maybe a steakhouse where there were other sixty-year-old guys with rinses. Miami must be loaded with places like that. And if he absolutely had to go to the other kind of place – the kind that he loved, with the Miriam Rosens and the gorgeous young litigators – see if there was anything legitimately worth exploring. If he came up with something, fine, but don't force it. And don't get humiliated so fast over every little setback.

But first Harry had to get off the balcony – a simple matter for most people, but not for Harry. He got to his feet carefully, keeping his legs bent at the knees, and tried not to stare down at the pavement. He had made that mistake earlier in the day and had seen some tropical trees below and had immediately started wondering if they could break his fall. Even if they could, he'd probably have to get into one of those halo braces designed by the woman he had spent all that time with.

Harry inched along until he got to the balcony door, which opened *toward* him, forcing him to step around it in a wide arc and to brush against the railing in order to get into the suite.

So Harry did all that, and even though he had lost some points – letting the balcony defeat him – he realized that he had probably (always *probably*, like the O.J. jurors) done the right thing. He poured himself a cup of coffee that he had made from the fresh Colombian beans he had ground himself – to show that, if necessary, he could be self-sufficient. Then he got the peach out of the refrigerator. He had bought it in a kosher store, and he wanted to see what was so special about it. So he bit into the kosher peach, and unless it was his imagination, it was the best peach he had ever tasted. So Harry drank the great coffee and ate the great peach and started to feel better, thinking the last three days were behind him.

"That's past," he said to himself, quoting a friend who appeared to have triumphed over a long illness. When the friend made that statement, he had accompanied it with a shoving motion, as if he were pushing aside a giant carton.

And it was past until it occurred to Harry that the condo he and Julie had bought on the beach had three balconies – one for every room, which was part of the sales pitch. And Harry had made the down payment before he realized how much trouble he had with balconies. So now he had three of them to worry about – unless he wanted to stay huddled in the middle of the apartment, which obviously defeated the purpose of having a condo in Miami, no matter what they said about getting too much sun.

Then Harry took hold of himself and decided it was too early to worry about the three balconies. The building was still under construction. All they had built was the lobby and the health club. It would take a year to get to his floor. (To "pour" his floor is the way they put it.) So there was plenty of time. And when he absolutely had to, he would deal with the balconies one at a time. Wasn't that what life was all about – taking it one balcony at a time?

If that wasn't a philosophy, he didn't know what was.

Harry would have to remember it, the next time someone suggested that he wasn't a serious man.

Mr. Wimbledon

ONCE MORE, into the country came Siegel, this time to a far-flung village in the Pacific Northwest, one he had flirted with as a vacationing youngster, wondering what it would be like to live there on a year-round basis. He was older, of course, but perhaps more formidable, accompanied as he was by Victoria St. John, who adored him when she could find the time. They rented a cheerful little cottage that may have been a shade too close to the lone Chinese restaurant in the area. Comforting to Siegel, the smell of hot prawns and garlic sauce was less of a treat for Victoria who enjoyed only one or two items on the menu, primarily the Dim Sum Parade. Each day, Siegel sent her out to inspect homes he had no thought of buying; it was his intention to spend a year in the area – playing a little tennis, also wading through dusty volumes in an effort to shore up his knowledge of history, finally bringing such figures as Talleyrand and Clemenceau into focus. He planned to plug up holes in his understanding of young America as well; he had no idea, to his shame, of why Shays – of Shays' Rebellion – had rebelled or, for that matter, why poor Bleeding Kansas bled.

But instead of practicing his ground strokes and sailing through Cotton Mather biographies, he found himself distracted by yet another favorite activity – looking for evidence of hostility to the Jews. Thus far, he hadn't come up with much, a pinched look here, a sidelong glance there. Nonetheless, he pressed on, convinced it was worth the effort.

After a week, the dry cleaner invited him to a pig roast at the dock. Siegel was about to take offense, then decided it was a friendly gesture, perhaps a tribute to the tremendous bill he and Victoria had racked up in such a short time, truly impressive for

only two people. The grateful dry cleaner had asked Siegel to sit
around and partake of a little pig with him. What was wrong with
that? And what was Siegel all of a sudden, kosher, with all the
spare ribs he had packed away in his time? So he let it pass. Shortly
thereafter, a toothless fisherman at the supermarket announced to
the checkout line that Walter Winchell had changed his name from
Louis Lipschitz.

"I don't blame him, do you?" he asked, then narrowed his
eyes and scanned the line, as if waiting for a show of hands.

Siegel prepared to lash out at the man, but held back. Though
it had come out of the blue, the question may well have been a
legitimate one. Who knows, perhaps it had nagged at the old-timer
on the rough seas, while he waited for marlin.

Should the great columnist, given the time and his choice of
profession, have stuck with Lipschitz?

Siegel, of course, had remained Siegel. He had achievements
in bulletproof sportswear. Why credit them to Atkinson or Seville,
two of the names he had flirted with? Nonetheless, he felt that
Winchell's choice was defensible. Had there been a vote among the
customers, he would have said so boldly. As it was, there was only
a generalized chuckling. Siegel fell in with it, an act of mild cowardice, since he didn't feel that jocular. Then he paid for his chicken
breasts and left. Once again, he had found nothing he could hang
his hat on.

Still, he pressed on in his search for behavior that was offensive to the Jews. If he couldn't find a little, what was the point of
being a Jew. Somewhere out there, they didn't like his people. All
he had to do was keep looking and he would be able to prove it.

In the city, Siegel never thought much about being a Jew. If
there was trouble, he could call other Jews. He certainly didn't
make this an issue when it came to dating. A woman could wave a
mezuzah in his face and he wouldn't notice it. It was a woman.
That was enough. Beyond the safety of the city's borders, it was
different. Years before, on Maine's craggy coast, Siegel had lived in
another community, shorn of his people. He recalled that in his

isolation he felt like a Jew the second he got up in the morning. This was true in bars and restaurants and when he took a leak. In his car he was a Jew. On occasion, he'd affected a folksy exterior; in actuality, he tiptoed along, ready at all times to be unmasked – forced to trade punches in the dirt with the person who had just caught him. He approached strangers with a bluff caution. Nor did he relax when he made friends. Israel might come up, provoking mixed emotions. God forbid, he'd have to take a stand. On several occasions, he'd made a study of the country's origins and legal right to exist. But the codicils and the Balfour Declaration kept fading on him. He'd read somewhere that London was a swamp when the Jews were in Palestine.

"London was a swamp," he'd say in argument, "when the Jews were in Palestine."

But that's all he knew. His lawyer, Brookline, was wise in the details of ancient Judea. But what was Siegel going to do, call the overworked attorney in the middle of the night when he was in a tight rhetorical spot? Just his luck, he'd get a bill.

Years had passed since Siegel had stood before a rural school board and in a strangulated voice asked: "Do you teach democratic values?"

A short, dark woman reprimanded him. "You're not the first one of your people we've had here." Again, his people.

Obviously, in the years that followed, the culture had changed. Jews were all over the place – high up in the Defense Department. There were laws that said you couldn't insult a Jew, except in the privacy of your home. Otherwise, you'd have to pay a fine. All of this enforced by tough assistant D.A.s of what else, the Jewish faith. Nobody even knew what a Jew looked like anymore. A case in point was Siegel himself, whose hair had become blond and flaxen over the years, though still revealingly kinky at the sides. This in contrast to the dark and sensuous Victoria St. John, from a distinguished WASP family, yet with a voluptuous body that had played no small part in their courtship, though of course he admired other qualities of hers as well. No longer did

Jews live through Koufax's arm or the achievements of Henny Youngman. General Ariel Sharon, arguably a *bullvun*, had thundered through the Middle East, demonstrating that you couldn't push Jews around anymore. They would come to your home and find you, even living under an assumed name in Terre Haute. Jews, when you could find them, stood tall, all, that is, except Siegel who hadn't lost a single relative to the camps but had been insulted once at a tennis club in Connecticut. Before leaving the lush grass courts, he'd raised a fist and vowed: "We don't forget."

So he continued his search, unable to relax unless he felt unwelcome. Could life be comfortable when there was no enemy at the gates? Siegel wasn't sure. Were there other Jews like him, still another lost tribe? He didn't know that many Jews and besides, he'd never asked.

Though Siegel tried to ferret out a little intolerance, the village held firm. The people were reserved, but was that grounds for an accusation? Should he call them together in Town Hall and say: "I'm sorry, but you've been a little reserved." When they'd lived among themselves for several hundred years? What were they supposed to do, run over and wash his feet? Because he'd decided to rent a cottage next to their only Chinese restaurant?

Then one night, in a local bar, just as he was about to throw in the towel, Siegel felt he'd struck paydirt. He could tell by the invitational curve of the fat man's arm that he was onto something.

Men with billowing volunteer ambulance jackets were bunched at the bar. Good-naturedly, they called each other asshole, forming their mouths into one. Waitresses, built low to the ground, smirked by. The special was sauerbraten. The stage was set. Siegel practically ran into the fat man's arms, and accepted a drink, so anxious was he to get underway. The man said he was Moon from the bait business. Siegel, of course, was Siegel; he was in defensive clothing. There was no need to tell the man he had made a killing in armored playsuits and that he was taking a year off to catch up on history, an old love. He could tell him that later. Quickly, it was established that both men grew up on Eastern Parkway, Moon insisting that his experience as a German-American in the early '40s was unique.

"You have no idea what it was like, being chased through the streets, not able to emerge from your apartment . . . and that song . . ."

Siegel, of course, was aware of the offending ballad, "In Der Fuhrer's Face." Sung with interspersed farting sounds, it satirized broadly the unthinking allegiance of Hitler's followers and seemed harmless enough at the time. Admittedly, he had never calculated its effect on a German-American fat boy at a formative stage of his life. Still, now that he had, what was he supposed to do, forget about that little matter with the Jews in Germany, call it a wash?

"It must have been rough," said Siegel.

Moon waved a disgusted arm. "It was awful," he said, his voice rising an octave.

Moon said he owned a house inland. Siegel was temporarily renting while he looked around.

"I live with my girlfriend, Victoria St. John."

As he said her name, he caught himself leaning forward as if waiting to be congratulated.

Moon ignored this. "Fuckin' Jews from Brooklyn," he said. "That's all they do is rent."

And there it was, out on the table, the fruits of a month-long search. Siegel congratulated himself on his diligence and the sensitivity of his antennae. Then he sat back, almost smug, prepared to savour his triumph. Yet oddly enough, the release he felt was vague and unsatisfactory. Perhaps there hadn't been enough foreplay. The "fuckin" was useful, of course, but the balance of the insult was hard to work with. What was he supposed to do, throw the man on the ground and spit in his face for suggesting that Jews rented? Of course they rented. That wasn't all they did. They also bought, as a man in a volunteers jacket was quick to testify.

"C'mon, Moon, they're grabbin' up the whole area."

"There you are," said Siegel, nodding his appreciation to the man, although not too vigorously, since, after all, he could hardly be considered a soulmate.

A Christ-like man at a table looked up from a slim volume and said: "You can't get published unless you're a Jew."

"What about Updike?" Siegel shot back and was prepared to buttress his argument with other examples if the ascetic-looking fellow persisted in the absurd argument.

"Jewish themes," said the fellow dismissively.

"What Jewish themes?" said Siegel, conveniently ignoring the excellent character, Bech.

Maddeningly, he felt he was being drawn into an argument in his old neighborhood. They might have been bickering over the Phillies' pennant chances. And the bar did have some characteristics of Eastern Parkway, an irony since for decades he hadn't been able to find one in the city, filled as it was now with rich Brazilians, another reason he had cleared out.

Surprisingly, the bartender, a tall slender fellow with a head of curls, responded well to the proceedings.

He beckoned Siegel to a back room and opened a safe. Expecting drugs or porn, Siegel instead got a look at Brad Van Pelt's helmet, on loan from a cousin in the area. Siegel asked if he could touch it, with sincerity, as it happened, since he had always admired the great linebacker who'd labored so heroically in a losing cause, only to be denied a Super Bowl triumph. When Siegel was finished playing with the helmet, the bartender leaned in close to him, shooting his eyes from side to side as if he were passing along a racing tip. In an overview of the evening, he said, "Hey-y-y, new bar . . . new guy . . . earn them spurs." Then, with several shakes of his tiny tush, he led Siegel back to the bar, immediately topping off Moon's drink in a show of impartiality.

"Anyone comes in here is lonely," said Moon, in a remark clearly directed at Siegel, although refusing to give him the courtesy of turning in his direction.

"Not necessarily," said Siegel, who took this as a personal

attack on his romance with Victoria, even though, disappointingly, she was back at Cavanaugh's Cottages, enjoying a sitcom lineup.

"Yes, necessarily," said Moon.

"Get your arm up here," said Siegel, theatrically clenching his teeth and pounding the bar.

"You'd lose," said Moon, with a sad wave of his hand.

"You're probably right," said Siegel, enclosed suddenly in the other man's gloom, as if it were a cologne.

Overtipping shamelessly, Siegel got up to leave.

Moon erupted in the style of a building superintendent, perhaps mimicking one who had chased him as a German fat boy.

"And don't you ever let me catch you bringing no book into a bar."

The new attack puzzled Siegel. Was this a reference to what he perceived to be Siegel's scholarly demeanor? He was in body armor. Where was the scholar? Did Moon know Jews who studied in bars? Siegel had cartons of books back at the cottage, but it was inconceivable that someone had phoned this information in to Moon. Be on the alert, Siegel's coming with books.

Nonetheless, the attack had to be answered: Siegel put a hand to his mouth, fell back in horror and, using a falsetto voice, said: "The people of the Book?" Then he did an Ali shuffle, threw some punches in the air and waltzed out of the bar in an absurd burst of conviviality.

But once outside, he felt sad, for himself, for the evening, for the paltry nature of his catch. If Moon with his tush and his renting was the new face of the enemy, the Jews might as well look for another profession. Where were the fresh young anti-Semites of yesteryear? Was it possible that he was lonely for the old Siegel, who would have been halfway out to the highway after such an evening, not sure if he should get guns or a psychiatrist? Or maybe round up Dong from the restaurant and go back and get them, picking up an old black jazz musician along the way for additional support. So that never again would anyone dare to take the position that Jews rented. The old Siegel slept with clenched fists and greeted each day as if he'd been shot out of a gun. He stuck wrenches in his tweed suit and went forth to avenge insults, sometimes over space at a counter. Was it possible to miss such a fellow? Of course. He missed his first hard-on, too. But such an individual would no longer be alive, having either shot himself or killed an innocent bystander. Fortunately, a doctor caught him in the nick of time. At a cost of five grand – and worth every penny of it, incidentally – he explained: "There *is* a little anti-Semitism out there." And just like that, Siegel popped quietly back into his slot, a useful member of society.

Now, as he whipped his Chrysler along the seacoast, he realized there was no one chasing him. Who had the time? Moon could barely get his ass off the bar stool. Who else was there? A waitress from the barley fields? What would she do when she caught him? Maybe Bunz, the bartender, would run after him and show him Y.A. Tittle's jock. He knew there was nothing to worry about. Eventually, death would step in and straighten him out. In the meanwhile, he slowed down. There was no need to fly along the Coast in this manner. He was safe and had to live with it.

Siegel had enjoyed a mystifying success in armored play suits. So confident was he that the line would be a disaster he sent Victoria to the stores to see how it was doing. She came back and reported overflow crowds. Even the footwear was selling, truly a surprise, considering how few people were shot in the feet. For the first time in his life, Siegel didn't have to worry about being tapped on the shoulder by the government. (There was a moral consideration. Unless sales were controlled, the wrong type of person might be able to defend himself. The industry wrestled with this issue.) Meanwhile, Siegel had bought a year. With frugality, perhaps more. So naturally, he rented. To buy would have been to define his feelings for Victoria.

The thought of his ladylove made him drive faster, although not too fast, since he was never sure what he would find when he got there. She hailed from a family of sleepwalkers. He might have to look for her in a tree. He wanted to spend eternity with Victoria, hand in hand, on separate but individual clouds – still, he was a little unsure of his feelings. Not once, for example, had she ever yelled at him. There was no evidence that she had ever yelled at anyone. Other men didn't exist for her – though he tried to arrange a little interest so he could be pissed off. She thanked him formally and promptly whenever they made love. A fresh cup of strong coffee stood ready for him each morning, although there was some question as to the long-term effect on his health. Her heart was his on a plate. Such a woman had to be watched.

So they lived impermanently, renting studios, waiting for something to happen. Something did happen and still they rented. Not that Siegel loved it. Take their current arrangement. Cavanaugh could sail in anytime he wanted to fix the plumbing. Or send his sons with bad skin to change a bulb. What if the youngsters caught Siegel fucking? It would have been nice to tell Cavanaugh to get lost. It bothered Siegel, too, that others in his field had waterfront property. He'd had a house once, too, but it slipped through his fingers. So he was careful to have nothing. Consequently, nothing could be taken away.

In a growing state of emergency, he ran up the stairs to their bedroom, shouldering his way through a barricade of food and magazines. Though Victoria came from vague wealth in Montana, she was reluctant to throw away anything. Bread crumbs had to be smuggled out in the dead of night. Also old copies of *Vanity Fair*.

Not surprisingly, Victoria's bed was empty. Instinct took him to Dong's restaurant – he didn't bother to check the roof. He'd already found her there and she tended not to repeat. Sure enough, there she sat, in her flannel nightgown, folding dumplings with Dong's daughters, not hurting a soul. Her legs gaped in the nightgown. What if Dong, for all his humanity, took a peek? Or worse, in the new culture, Dong's daughters? Was there any guarantee that Victoria would wake up in time?

Sally, the prettiest daughter, shot a look at Victoria, rotating a finger at her own temple to connote an unbalanced state. Then, moist-eyed, she pressed her face against the window pane and said: "Something's wrong, Siegel, something's missing in my heart. I keep waiting and waiting for it to happen, but it never does. Do you think it ever will?"

Though Siegel was tenaciously faithful to Victoria, he'd considered the actress-y Sally, then erased the thought. His only experience with an Asian woman had ended, to his shame, when he pulled back his friend Han's seal black waist-length hair to reveal the jaw of a Mongol warrior.

Siegel diplomatically ducked the girl's question, then scooped Victoria up in his arms. He had met her when he was distributing free vests to the endangered workers at an abortion clinic in the Carolinas. They weren't top-of-the-line items, but they would be of some use; it was better than going bare-chested against pickets. Back then, the vest weighed more than she did. Now Victoria had some heft to her. Lifting her, he felt a pain in the fifth metacarpal. A few more pounds and he'd have a back condition. Still, he loved the feel of her rough nightgown on his face. No one smelled as much like a person as she did. On an adjacent lawn, the Cavanaughs snapped open beers. He carried Victoria to their bed. Before she took her stroll, she'd plumped up the pillows on his side, folded his pajamas and left a note that said: "For Captain Cozy." She was a sleep chatterer, too. Holding out a small hand, palm upward, she had called for reason from anti-abortion hecklers. It had been drilled into him; don't rouse a sleepwalker. But the hand got to him and he whispered: "Let's buy a place here. I can't explain it, but there's something about this area I like."

The next morning, to show he wasn't afraid of anyone, Siegel ordered eggs at the local diner. The sauerbraten boys were bunched in a corner. A waitress, Dawn, from the night before, slid hotcakes at them. When his order was a little slow in coming out, Siegel was offended. What point were they trying to make? That Jews ate too many eggs? Is that what ailed America? Maybe they should be taught a lesson and have to wait for their eggs. The thoughts were involuntary. Some day he would have to stop thinking that way. Did he really believe that people had nothing to do except worry about Jews? The second they got up in the morning? That they didn't have to make a living, like the poor waitress who had to draw strength from her stocky legs so she could work the breakfast shift? Siegel had time to worry about Jews, not them.

Outside, Siegel saw Moon with a shopping bag, asking himself a question in the rain. In the bar, his fatness had a pinky ring elegance to it. Now, in the daylight, he wore ear flaps and a short Mackinaw jacket that called unnecessary attention to his spectacular tush. He might have been the kind of fat fellow who stood in shopping malls with his mother, a religious fanatic. Moon let a bus go by, then came inside and said he felt Siegel had overreacted the night before. Siegel denied the charge, but with a show of graciousness, asked Moon to join him for a cup of coffee. Moon accepted, emptying the contents of his bag on the table, a combination of fishnets, chicken wire and possibly some felt from his last Mackinaw, all formed into what was supposed to be a vest. Siegel pushed it away from his eggs and wondered, what did he do, stay up all night to create this concoction? When he heard Siegel was in the business? And after pretending he didn't notice?

"Would you mind looking this over?" asked Moon.

"Not at all," said Siegel, who had already decided it had no commercial application. Still, the garment had a certain rough integrity to it. Siegel had been wrong before, on his own playsuits. Maybe it could be featured in a country line.

"I'll send it to the lab," said Siegel.

"Thanks," said Moon. "Last night I didn't know where you were coming from."

"Others have made that mistake," said Siegel, not sure if this was true.

Moon went back to the rain. Siegel wondered if he had dressed pathetically for effect. Also, he was slightly disappointed. Their first encounter had been promising. He had expected a lot more from the man.

Victoria was tentative in showing him the house. Why should she have her hopes dashed again? But as they walked up the driveway, Siegel said: "I'll take it, I'll take it," in part because he didn't hate it, but also because Moon had branded him as a renter. What began as a slur ended on a happy note, with Siegel being bullied into a house that was probably good for him.

The house itself had been moved from place to place. At one point, it was spotted in west Texas. The owner, transferred frequently, loved it so much he took with him. Finally, he dropped dead and had no further use for it. Like an Army brat, the house was adaptable. Stick in a window, tear off a wing, the house didn't mind. It was happy to be a house. The closing costs cut deeply into Siegel's savings. Already he could see his year off had been cut to seven months. Instead of covering the history of Venice doge by doge, he'd have to go for broad strokes. Victoria brought antique rugs out of storage which were useful, although frankly he wouldn't have minded if she asked her family to come across with a few dollars. But he was too shy. In the city, they had virtually licked each other's internal organs, but about money, he was shy. That and asking her to lie next to him in the next grave. She was younger. It wasn't fair to tie her up that way. If she volunteered, that was another thing. He'd be happy to have her aboard. Maybe that's what love was, not pressuring the other person into the next grave. Taking your chances on a stranger.

A homeowner now, Siegel nonetheless remained loyal to Dong, even though his sauces had gone off badly; no doubt he was distracted by his inability to provide a satisfying social life for his daughters, although Sally had made inroads among woodcutters. One night, Siegel sat next to a family of four whose lives were closely intertwined with that of a club. Their sweaters were embroidered with club insignia; throughout the meal they discussed club affairs. A new member had attempted to sell insurance on the links.

"At the club?" said the shocked wife.

"I'm afraid so, Gail," said her silver-haired husband.

From time to time, the head of the family looked around to make sure there was someone in the place who didn't belong to the club and couldn't get in. This, of course, could only mean Siegel, since he was the only other person in the restaurant. Unless you wanted to include Dong who couldn't get in either, at least until he became a franchise.

"Well, I guess we'd better be getting back to the club," said the father, scrutinizing the check carefully.

"Yes, Dad," said one daughter, "Our dates are waiting for us."

"At the club," said the other.

At one time, Siegel would have been shattered that he didn't belong to such an organization, even though he had no idea of the facilities. But this was the new Siegel. He did the excluding. The fact that he was alone all the time was another story.

Still, the encounter put him in the mood for a little exercise. Victoria, with frail ankles, was less interested, but she found a club for him, one that anyone could join; as a result, it had no members. Alone on a high promontory, Siegel staged furious tennis rallies with the ball machine. One day he played the owner's son, a bewildered child who beat the shit out of him anyway. Then the wind shifted violently in Siegel's favor, giving him a chance. He won a few games, then became aware of a voice from his old neighborhood, breaking his concentration. On the next court was a woman with orange hair.

"What kind of backhand is that?" she asked her partner, a silent man with powerful legs that looked as if they'd crossed the Negev.

"Oh, for Christ's sakes," she said, a moment later, "I can't hit a goddamned thing."

Siegel tried to ignore her, although a process had begun that he couldn't control. As he prepared for a serve, she excused herself and ran onto his court.

"I'll only be a second," she said, then knelt with chunky dimpled knees and fished around for a ball that had her initials on it.

"There," she said, when she'd found it. "Was that so terrible?"

"It was an important point," said Siegel.

"And there'll be plenty of others."

Siegel tried to stay calm, telling himself the game was unimportant. What would the kid do if he won, announce it on the six o'clock news?

Siegel resumed the game, then saw the woman sit down on a bench and throw a leg behind her head. Never before had he seen someone stretch a tendon that way. He was powerfully tempted to take a good look, but felt it would be a concession and pressed on.

A few minutes later, she interrupted again.

"There's such a thing as etiquette," said Siegel.

"Oh well, excuse me, Mr. Wimbledon."

Then she called out, "Si, would you come over here and help me look. They've got quite a few of our balls here."

"Maybe you should bring an accountant," said Siegel.

"Fuck you," said the man, then walked in a little circle, snorting at the ground.

"Fuck your mother," was Siegel's less than rapier-like response.

Nonetheless, it was a remark he had always wanted to try out.

Siegel was afraid of Si's legs. Nor was he confident about his own energy level. Still, he advanced toward the man who came to meet him.

"It's not worth it, Si," said the woman. "If that's his style, you'll never change him."

Both men raised their Prince Charles Classics at the same time. Siegel heard a familiar voice cry out "Mocky," a word dredged up from his childhood, like a dirty animal in a cellar. He was shocked when he realized the voice was his own, but also gratified that he had finally found the enemy.

The Reversal

ANATOLE HAD BEEN SEEING DR. GOLD – on and off – for several decades. Gold had made a mistake or two. Once, almost unforgivably, he had told Anatole that he had a secure position in the second tier of architects. And on more than one occasion Gold had referred to a book by the comedian Sid Caesar as "literature." But in the overall, Gold had helped Anatole a great deal. He had seen his patient through a hellish divorce, effectively making light of it when Anatole threatened to throw himself off a bridge. Gold was there for Anatole through his gall bladder surgery and virtually held his hand when a partner sued him for defamation. Gold's office was in Long Island, an hour's drive from Manhattan. When Anatole lived in a neighboring town, it was easy to get to the doctor's office. Anatole lived in Manhattan now. Yet, such was Gold's importance to him that once a week he drove out to Rockville Centre to see his old psychiatrist.

Anatole's life was on a comfortable track. At age forty-five, he lived alone in a four-story walk-up in Chelsea. An Irish setter kept him company as he worked. His small business was humming along, He had no shortage of friends. Thank God his health was highly decent.

One morning, after he'd eaten breakfast and polished off the *Times*, the downstairs buzzer rang.

"It's Melvin Gold here. Do you mind if I come up?"

"Of course not," said Anatole, who was surprised, if not shocked, by the unusual visit. "Wait till you hear the click and then open the door quickly."

Gold was breathing heavily when he entered the apartment. It was clear he wasn't accustomed to climbing stairs. The psychiatrist was a sixty-year-old man of medium height with a swelling paunch. His long hair was gray and his moustache – which Anatole had never cared for – drooped a bit at the corners. No doubt it was designed to take the focus away from his large teeth.

"I hope I didn't catch you at a bad time," said Gold.

"Of course not," said Anatole, who'd been preparing to do the proposal for a renovation and hated being thrown off schedule.

Overdressed for the season, Gold removed his topcoat and took a seat in Anatole's favorite chair.

"Would you like some coffee?" asked Anatole.

"No, no . . ." said Gold. "The caffeine."

"I can make some decaf. . . ."

"That's worse," said Gold, not bothering to explain. He was still out of breath.

"How can I help you?" asked Anatole.

It seemed a ridiculous question. He realized that as he said it. How could he possibly help the distinguished psychiatrist?

"These stairs," said Gold, breathing hard. "Don't get me wrong," he said defensively. "I can cycle for an hour. . . . It's lifting my own weight that's a hassle. . . ."

"Oh hell," he said, as if he'd lost a debate. "Maybe I'll have it checked. . . ."

"It's always a good idea," said Anatole, who had just skipped his own physical.

"I've probably caught you off guard. And I'm aware that this visit is against the norm. Usually, when I'm in a shitstorm, I see Gussie Lanzer, a Viennese Jungian. But she must be a hundred and five now and frankly I'm tired of talking to a stone wall. If I get five words out of her, it's a victory. To cap it off, she's promoted herself to four hundred an hour. When we started, she was twenty-five."

Anatole was reminded that he was behind in his payments to Gold. He owed him five hundred dollars – but at least it was for two visits.

"But this has got nothing to do with money," Gold continued, "although I know, I know, there's some denial there. I've remort-gaged the townhouse and it's freed up quite a bit of cash. Still, if I look at that middle European pruneface one more time, I'll get nauseous. So I thought I'd change the game plan and try the unor-thodox. It's worked for me before. I once got sound advice from a building superintendent. Pure gold, actually. That's what brings me here. I thought I'd see you."

"I'm flattered," said Anatole. And apart from the disruption in his schedule, he was. "But what are my qualifications?"

"For one thing, you're no dummy. And you've been around the block. You're more qualified than you think. And you know your customer. How long have we been in business? Twenty years? We've been through a lot. Hell, if we're not friends now, Anatole, we'll never be. May I call you 'Anatole?'"

"Please. . . ."

"Good. You can call me 'Mel.'"

Anatole thought he'd risk a question. He was flying blind, but for a split second, he enjoyed this strange reversal of roles.

"So what's on your mind," he asked. Awkwardly, he added, "Mel?"

"Where do I start? All right, I might as well come clean. In a nutshell, my life is shit. Nothing works anymore. My profession, the marriage, my kids. . . . I always thought that at this stage of my life, I'd give my patients a hug, say goodbye and circle the globe. But Glo is tied up with her own practice now, treats a whole flock of Bangladeshis. I've always enjoyed traveling, but suddenly I'm afraid to go it alone. China's been on the agenda for years. But what if I fainted in Shanghai? Had an oracular migraine attack in Katmandu? And what were all my trips about anyway? Those seminars? You think I went to Frankfurt to lecture? Or to see the cathedrals? Half the time I was chasing pussy. Spend a little time in the Old City, maybe catch an opera to cover my ass, then start cruising. But let's say I take a trip now and I get lucky. Some hot lit-tle widow hears I'm a shrink and shows interest. What do I do, pop a pill and pray that it clicks in? Let's say she changes her mind. Or I misread her intentions. What do I do then, walk around Stuttgart with a lonely hard-on?

"I did enjoy walking," Gold continued, reflectively. "Any place, as long as I hadn't seen it before. All that *adventure*. My favorite word if that fellow Lipton ever asks me on his show. But I've got a curvature now. I take ten steps and there's a piano on my back. This morning I arrived in the Apple, bright and early. My tongue was hanging out with the possibilities. But I can't god-damned walk. They don't have benches. What am I supposed to do, circle Harlem in a pedicab?"

It didn't take a professional to see that Gold was drowning in self-pity.

"How about Glo?" Anatole asked, trying to strike a positive note. "Your wife," he added quickly, as if Gold might miss the connection.

"Good point," said Gold. "Glo's got the Bangladeshis on the couch from nine in the morning to six at night. By the time she gets home, she's all fagged. It's a cigarette, *Law and Order* and off to bed. She still wets my whistle, don't get me wrong . . . but she's got no time for me. And what the hell could I offer her anyway? She's heard my back story. And let's face it, she takes a drink. Most nights I have to cover her up – all sprawled out like the homeless – get the lamplight out of her eyes. She's worth the trip, though. I'm not saying that. But if only I could have her attention, full time. Sail her up the Nile, clean and sober. My girl again. Wouldn't that be something?"

His eyes teared up at the thought.

"Would you like a tissue?" asked Anatole.

"Of course not," Gold snapped. But he cooled down quickly and accepted one. "You probably want to know about the kids?"

"It had crossed my mind."

"Number One Son lives off the land in Georgia, kills his food with a stun gun. He's probably aiming at me – claims I smacked him around when he was toddling. My other son's a gem. Builds houses in Morristown, but he won't take five minutes off to smell the coffee. Came out to buy me lunch last week and I caught him looking at his watch, like the first Bush."

"And your patients? You've helped me. I'm sure there are others."

"Accountants? Tortured accountants? Shall we not yank my chain."

"Any hobbies?" asked Anatole, who realized instantly that he had made a mistake. Gold would choke on the banality of the question. Anatole almost did himself.

"You mean folk dancing?" said Gold. He looked at Anatole as if he were a member of an alien species. "Is that what you'd like me to do? How about basket-weaving? Or collecting. That's a good one. Why don't I start collecting mouse figurines? Would that make you happy?"

"Sorry if I offended you. I saw some artifacts in your office. I thought perhaps you went on digs."

"Dig my own grave, that's more like it. Those *objets* you saw on my desk. It's my homage to Freud. The good doctor's second love was anthropology – but you probably knew that."

"More or less," said Anatole.

"Maybe I was showing off a little. But this is not about digs," said Gold in frustration. "Can we not talk about digs?"

"Forget digs," said Anatole gently.

"Good," said the psychiatrist." It's the here and now that gives me grief, Anatole. Lindsay *Lo*han? Kevin Federline? Rummi? Brownie? 50 Cent, for Christ's sake. Where do *I* come in, Anatole? I drove off the highway and I can't get back on? What on God's earth is happening? Wonkette? Canoodling? Tonsil Hockey? Paris Fucking Hilton? I ask you, Anatole – Bingo Bloody Gubelmann? I know there's no second act. But where's the third?"

He leaned forward with genuine longing in his eyes.

"What do you make of this? What's getting me down? What's it all about, Anatole?"

"What do you think?"

"What do *I* think? Now there's a question for you. What do *I* think. I don't think anything. What in bloody hell do you think I'm doing here?"

"What if I showed up in your office and dumped a package – such as the one you've described – in *your* lap?"

"'Dumped' is good," said Gold. "I like 'dumped.'"

"But what would you do?"

Gold appeared to ignore the question. He sat quietly, staring straight ahead, as if he was watching a pill dissolve in a glass of water. Then he took a deep breath.

"Well, for one thing," he said, "I'd tell you to get off your ass and consider what you've got. You're a revered figure – and not just in Rockville Centre. Your influence spills out in all directions. You lecture in Oslo every year. Ask the Norwegians what they think of you. I know, I know, it's Norway, but they've got some awfully decent people over there . . . . Your wife adores you – she's preoccupied at the moment, but she'll come round. Basically, you're her guy. Who do you think gives her the strength to deal with those East Asians? Your patients are accountants? What are they, lepers? Here's some news for you. An accountant can have a heavy heart, too. And ask them for *their* opinion of you. They'd be happy to line up and kiss your feet, not to speak of your fat ass.

"Take a fucking walk. So you'll limp a little. It's not a death sentence. And *go* to Shanghai. What if you do get a migraine? The city's been around for a thousand years. You think they won't know how to treat a migraine? You've got a full plate. ENJOY YOUR GODDAMNED LIFE."

The two men sat in silence, Gold breathing heavily.

"Thank you," he said.

"Not at all," said Anatole.

"You're very good."

"I doubt that."

"Trust me . . . and what do I owe you for this visit?"

"It's on the house."

"That's enormously kind," said Gold, getting up to leave. "Now what about you?"

"I'm fine."

"Medication?"

"Actually, I'm running low on lorazepan."

"I'll phone in a prescription. And I'll expect to see you on Thursday in Rockville Center."

"Four-thirty. I'll be there."

Gold put on his topcoat, walked to the door, then hesitated.

"What if I wanted to pop 'round and see you – for another 'session'?"

"That can be arranged. Just call ahead and give me some lead time."

"I'd insist on paying."

"We can work it out."

"It's highly unlikely," said Gold. "It was just a thought."

He opened the door.

"Unless, of course, I happen to be in the neighborhood."

An Affair

SHE FELT it was her literary prominence that appealed to him.

He claimed it was her smoky voice, and her air of having attended good schools.

He was ten years younger than she was.

She was close to hysteria when he arrived late for their first rendezvous and admitted openly that he had been with a college friend – and slept with her – and then said goodbye to her forever.

She had no reason to doubt this.

She was overcome, and wept, at the first sight of his naked body.

Their affair, which was intensely sexual, began officially (as she saw it) when she whispered two words to him: "Be rougher."

His first attempts were mannered, but he quickly became skilled at it.

They would meet at her apartment, which he found cold and which he – of all people – made livable with a number of purchases. Rugs and paintings.

He was a venture capitalist, though he rarely spoke of it, and lived with his parents.

In the year they spent together, she could not recall a single day during which they had failed to make love.

In July and August, they remained in the city and enjoyed having it to themselves.

A song (with patently absurd lyrics) was in the air and became the backdrop of their affair.

She considered her lovemaking spontaneous, without thought or calculation. In truth, she had certain skills, the use of her teeth, for example, on his penis and scrotum.

Though she had the other, he preferred that she wear plain cotton underwear.

He enjoyed watching her masturbate.

She enjoyed watching him watch her – but only now and then.

He locked her out of the apartment one night. She stood shivering and naked in the corridor. Tacitly, she had agreed to this. A neighbor, disappointingly, ignored the spectacle. When he finally opened the door for her, predictably, they made love with a fury.

They kept raising the ante, not out of boredom, but for the adventure.

She gave him a leather crop. For his rides in the park, but not entirely.

As a gift, she offered him a girlfriend, but on condition that she be present. He accepted – once – and they survived the experience.

He often slept with his face buried in her vagina.

When the sex was most intense, he complained of feeling pain and she realized she's been clamping down on his penis as he came. Perhaps to ward off pregnancy. She stopped doing that.

Never once did he say he loved her.

Nor did she say that she loved him.

Although she did.

For a time.

And she was confident he loved her.

He took her to have cocktails with his parents. She could see the hatred in his mother's eyes – and the weary understanding in his father's.

They took only one vacation together. As they stood on a hill and looked out on Charlotte Amalie Harbor, she felt a need to suck his penis.

She often felt that need.

She wrote a novella in five days, as part of the vacation.

But it wasn't any good.

At a party, her editor made a snide comment about his prominent nose. She changed editors. But it continued to bother her.

Though he could do the *Times* crossword puzzle in a flash, he was not terribly verbal. That troubled her as well. What he did for the most part was to look at her in silence and try to anticipate her every need. As if he were a nurse and she had been ill.

Which she had been, in a sense, having walked out on a troubled marriage.

But she had recovered. And begun to notice other men. Some were closely allied to her professionally. Others were not.

She broke off their affair suddenly, perhaps with some cruelty, as if she had lost confidence in a book she was writing and set it aside. She said she wanted to try again with her husband. Which wasn't true.

He took her decision poorly, sending back the first editions of her novels that she had given him. Mutilated.

He begged her, literally on hands and knees, to stay with him. Behavior that sealed his fate.

She saw him only once again, months later, by chance – at a diner. They each had a cup of coffee. She asked if she could call him for dinner.

He agreed to this, but said that he was seeing someone, therefore it could only be for dinner.

She was offended by the assumption that she wanted more (she had) and did not call him.

Years passed.

She had always felt that she would have other affairs, of equal or greater sexual intensity. She felt it was her due.

But this did not come about.

At a certain point, she came to realize that it never would.

Joined at the Hip

"IF YOU WANT TO GET SPRUNG, tell 'em you're lonely for your dear old mum."

The line of dialogue, which was intended to be spoken by a demoniacal guard, and followed by a cackle, caused the prisoner to sit up on his flimsy metal chair and to come out of his trance.

I had chosen the line deliberately. It existed in a novel written by the prisoner, one published before he had broken through to a wide audience. You'd need to have been a devoted reader of Monroe Gillis to have remembered the line. None was more devoted than I was.

I recognized him from the photograph on his book jackets – and I had attended one of his talks at a mystery writers' convention in Saratoga. He was – and continued to be – a raffishly handsome man whose looks were somewhat out of joint with the times. Slender, somewhat delicately put together, he wore a small moustache and his profile was a classic one. He had the look of a minor matinee idol of decades past. (Indeed, a feminist, who disapproved of the portrayal of women in his books, had denounced him during his talk in Saratoga as a "poor, poor creature of the '40s" before storming out of the auditorium.) Gillis was sixty-three. Even in drab prison clothing and with a three-day growth of beard, he still managed to throw off a careless charm.

I was not the detective assigned to the case. But as a diehard Gillis fan, and with a reputation in the department of being a "culture vulture," I had little difficulty obtaining a permission to visit the distinguished prisoner.

The murder he had almost eagerly confessed to committing was adjudged, by several veteran detectives, to be a particularly vicious one. The victim was Dmitri Slotkin, a theatrical producer, mainly of lightweight drawing room comedies, imported from London. He had been killed by a single thrust, or chopping blow to the bridge of the nose, the weapon a Filipino "fighting knife" with a 14-inch blade and an ebony handle. In the hyperbolic report of the arresting officer, the victim's head had been split open "like a coconut." It was the celebrated writer himself who had made the call to the police. He had then calmly taken a seat beside the victim, but not before – and this was an odd detail – looping his belt through that of Slotkin – thereby attaching himself to the dead producer.

After his virtually immediate confession, he had been arrested and then arraigned and now – in a holding cell that seemed even more cheerless than most – awaited sentencing. I was curious to learn what circumstance it was that had driven a distinguished author and a man of great sophistication (not a word I throw around lightly) to an act of such homicidal fury.

Having established my bona fides with the quotation of a line in an obscure book of his, Gillis, a natural storyteller, seemed only too happy to discuss his unfortunate case.

"Slotkin and I were doing a play together, you know," said Gillis, setting the scene as if we had both settled in for an exchange of stories beside a campfire.

I recalled vaguely seeing an item to that effect in the press and hoping for selfish reasons it was only public relations fluff. If true, it would have meant an interruption in the regular flow of Gillis novels, an unhappy development for his legion of fans. Then, too, I was aware that authors of greater stature than Gillis – Henry James, Scott Fitzgerald, as examples – had broken their backs on the frustrating and unforgiving shoals of the theatre world.

"When did you first meet?" I asked.

"Two years ago," he said, then paused and corrected himself. "Two and a half, to be truthful. I think of it as two and a half years torn out of my life."

He had been pacing the length of the cell as he spoke, but this last admission seemed to drain his strength. He sat down heavily, as if to recover.

"I'd never attempted a play before, but I'd always enjoyed the theatre and thought, as a change of pace, I'd take a try at one. I was apprehensive when the finished piece was circulated by my agents. Much to my surprise and delight, Dmitiri Slotkin, whose name I recognized, called and said he wanted to produce the play. We arranged to meet at his offices in mid-Manhattan. I found him to be a bluff and charming man, even by the standards of theatre – a world in which charm – or what passes for it – is as abundant as running water. He seemed genuinely happy to have been offered the play and said he planned to mount it that very season. We would have no difficulty, he assured me, in finding a director. 'I can get you twenty,' he said, with a snap of his fingers. He pointed out that his approach to producing was to concentrate on a single play each season. Mine was the one he had chosen. No backers would be required. 'When you have Dmitri Slotkin,' he said confidently, 'you don't need anyone else.' And in the months – and then years that followed – he was to repeat this statement like a mantra."

"Didn't that strike you as unusual?" I asked Gillis.

It was common knowledge that the cost of mounting a play in Manhattan had become astronomical. Typically, a producer would take on as many as four or five partners to lighten the burden.

"I didn't think much about it at all. Slotkin had a substantial reputation. I felt I was in very good hands and took the production of my play as a given. I even allowed myself to think ahead to a celebratory opening night party, perhaps at Sardi's, thereby assuring myself of a small niche in a grand theatrical tradition. It was only as I prepared to leave his office that I was thrown off stride by the question he posed to me."

"What is your play about?" he asked.

"In retrospect, I can see that this should have thrown up a flag. How could he possibly produce a play whose meaning escaped him? Nonetheless, I did what I could to answer him. At the heart of the work was a young man's having to choose between art and commerce. Since this did not sound particularly flashy, I took a minute or two to relate the events of the story as they would unfold on stage. He considered this, and after stroking his beard thoughtfully, he clapped me on the back and said: 'No matter . . . We are now joined at the hip.' This was yet another phrase I was to hear more than once in the months to come."

I thought back to the crime scene, as described in the police report.

"That would account for the belt business. . . ."

He smiled, as if relishing his handiwork.

"It was a touch I couldn't resist . . . theatrical. . . ."

Obviously, the play never opened. If it had, I was enough of a theatregoer to have known about it.

"So he disappointed you. . . ."

"That's a mild way of putting it. It was as if I'd been lured into some kind of shell game. Directors, the few who expressed interest, were hired by Slotkin and subsequently fired. There were a series of readings for people who were obviously potential backers, although Slotkin insisted they were 'friends' who might be useful in getting the word out that a hit was in the making. Casting and rehearsal dates were announced, then canceled. Several seasons passed, during which time Slotkin managed to produce three cabaret-style evenings, two small-scale musicals, several dramatic readings, and one huge turkey of an alleged comedy. I was invited to attend them all, and I did so, as a courtesy. One was more tedious than the other, which only increased my irritation. . . ."

I hadn't seen a Monroe Gillis mystery novel in the stores for several years – and I guessed, correctly, that during this period, he had set aside his work on the novels.

"That was the worst of it," he said, confirming my suspicion. "I was so convinced that the play would eventually go on that I completely neglected the other. Good God, I could have written three novels in that time. When I think of the loss of income alone. . . . So you can imagine my feelings when Slotkin showed up at my studio one day and announced that he was unable to find any support for the play and would have to withdraw as a producer. He claimed it was one of the most painful decisions he'd ever had to make – and assured me that he would read any future efforts of mine with interest."

"Do you feel he deliberately misled you?"

"I doubt that it was deliberate. I think he had some vague interest in my play. But what he seemed to value more was being associated with me. I realize this sounds presumptuous, but I kept hearing reports of this. He would take people aside and tell them that he was doing the first theatre piece by the world-renowned mystery writer, Monroe Gillis. . . . He dined out on that . . ."

"Still . . . you must have been infuriated when he dropped the play."

"I suppose I should have been, but oddly enough, that was not the case. Was I upset? Of course. But I have strong recuperative powers. I knew that after a brief mourning period, I'd be able to start up the engine and go back to what I do best. And to be frank, I had become unsure about the play. It may be that I am simply not cut out to be a playwright and ought to leave that field to those who are to the theatre born. Then, too, the sheer chutzpah of the man showing up at my studio to deliver his hideous message no doubt caught me off guard. There didn't seem to be any point in shouting at him, berating him. I simply could not work up a proper level of outrage to fit the situation."

But of course, obviously, he had. And we had come to the whole point of my visit. I tried to phrase my question delicately.

"What was it that finally . . . set you off?"

Gillis put his hand to his forehead in concentration, as if he wanted to get it exactly right, for some sort of record.

"Soon after Slotkin left my office, having dropped his bomb, I took myself off to the Caribbean. I had decided that what I needed for a fresh start was a change of scenery. It was a strategy that had worked for me before. Sunshine, those wonderful rum drinks, a little blackjack, and in short order I'd be off and running on a new project.

I've never had a shortage of ideas. . . . It occurred to me that I might do a mystery novel that would make use of some of the scenes in my abandoned play. No point wasting them. I chose a small hotel in Barbados. After a day or two of idling around, I jumped in and tried an opening scene, which came across as being forced and stilted. The theatre experience had evidently taken more out of me than I was willing to admit. Rather than get into a state, I set the work aside and walked out to the patio which was beside the hotel pool. It was a lovely day. As I looked around for a comfortable spot, I noticed a young woman who was stretched out on a chaise lounge. Though I tried to be discreet, I could not stop staring at her, the reason being that she was one of the most unforgivably beautiful women I had ever seen. Other than to say that she was fair-haired and that her features were flawless, I won't attempt to describe her. I lack to power to do so."

There was no reason to doubt Gillis' judgment in this area. He had spent a good number of years in Hollywood as a screenwriter and had been exposed to more than his share of lovely women. Several of his wives had been legendary in this category.

He continued: "As she got to her feet, I half hoped to detect some flaw in her appearance. I had come to the island for a specific purpose and I did not need this distraction. But the Gods had apparently not quite finished toying with me. If her face was perfection, her tall slender body and her totally unselfconscious movements were even more so. By current standards . . . that thong business . . . the two-piece bathing suit she wore was modestly cut, all of which had a reverse and almost unbearably erotic appeal.

"What set off her appearance even more dramatically was the odd-looking individual who followed her to the pool and seemed to be her companion. He had a good height, but his shoulders and chest were sparrow-like, his stomach huge, and his legs spindly and shapeless. I would prefer not to comment on the scattered patches of hair on his head and his womanish breasts. He might have been thrown together out of random body parts. What was most disturbing is that they seemed to get along remarkably well, his disagreeable appearance not seeming to matter to her in the least. He stood at the edge of the pool, barking out remarks to her in some strange tongue that I couldn't quite make out. It seemed to be their private code. Whatever it was he was saying seemed to delight her. She swam for a bit with a grace that was heart-breaking. And then, before the fates could intervene, he hurled himself into the pool and the two went splashing and cavorting about and having the time of their lives. At one point, unconscio-nably, she leapt upon his spindly shoulders, to be joyously carried, piggy-back, from one end of the pool to the other, her crotch pressed trustingly and maddeningly against his neck."

He took a deep breath as if to recover from the unsavory image.

"All of this struck me as being horrendously unfair. The mis-match between them – unnoticed by her – had to be an affront to nature. After she had left the pool and dried herself with a towel, she lay upon her stomach and lowered her top, allowing her sur-prisingly heavy breasts to swing free. It had crossed my mind that he might be a cousin or some sort of freakish sibling, but the casual and intimate manner in which he spread lotion on her shoulders and the backs of her legs led me to believe that they were lovers – no matter how appalling the prospect might be.

"I cannot tell you how offended I was by this ungodly cou-pling and how much I wanted that woman. For my own purposes, of course, but also to redress some awful blunder in the natural order. Under normal circumstances, it would not have presented a huge problem for me to meet her . . . or perhaps I should say to meet them. There weren't that many guests at the hotel. I would simply have introduced myself, asked if they were from the States and what had brought them to the hotel. Something innocuous along those lines – and with a pretense of being interested in the two of them. I might have asked her friend what sort of work he did and quickly gotten it across that I was a writer of mysteries. Perhaps they'd heard of me. And I'd insist on presenting them with a signed copy of my latest novel. I made sure to carry several in my valise for this very purpose. This might, inevitably, lead to the three of us having a drink in the evening, perhaps going to dinner. And then slowly, I would ease closer to her, gently and perhaps imperceptibly nudging her friend or companion aside. I am not suggesting that this would necessarily have led to my going to bed with her, although the odds would be in my favor. What I'm saying is that I was determined to have her and that somehow I would do whatever it took to achieve this – charm, wheedle, cajole, if necessary bull my way into the situation until I had her. I had been able to pull off this sort of thing before. . . ."

"But not this time. . . ."

"I had every opportunity," said Gillis, not disagreeing with me. "That first day at the pool, she looked over at me on one occasion in a friendly manner. Following her lead, the friend or companion, or whatever he was, even threw a ghastly smile in my direction. There were so few people at the hotel . . . they may have even been mildly curious about me, wondering why I was there alone. . . . And yet somehow I could not bring myself to approach them. Instead, I spent a miserable night thinking about her, obsessing about her and how much I wanted her. It became worse for me the following day when I encountered them once again at the pool. He was reading *The Financial Times*, the clod, and she was holding a slim volume of the work of Siegfried Sassoon, one of the few poets I admire and whose work is familiar to me. I could have simply come up to her and recited aloud his haunting line: 'To mock the riddled corpses round Bapaume.' My God, how much better an opportunity could a man ask for . . ."

"And yet . . . ," I said, as he paused and seemed to berate himself.

"I let that opportunity slip as well. . . . That night, I saw them having dinner on the terrace of the hotel dining room. With a fresh tan, set off against her white gown, she was more ravishing than before. We'd been together, so to speak, for several days now in the thinly populated little hotel. By this time, there would have been something odd, or even rude, about my not speaking to them – even if my intentions were less predatory. After fortifying myself with several glasses of Merlot, I polished up a few Sassoon anecdotes . . . and finally approached them. They looked up at me, somewhat expectantly. My 'adversary' half rose from his chair to greet me, somewhat less clumsily than I would have imagined. I nodded politely in their direction, hesitated as I came alongside their table, fully intending to speak to them – and then maddeningly found myself walking out of the restaurant or, to put it correctly, it was as if someone was walking me out of the restaurant . . . and into the lobby. . . ."

"And that was it?"

"The whole of it."

"You never saw either of them again. . . ."

"Never. . . ."

"You returned to New York. . . ."

"The very next day. . . ."

"Went to Slotkin's office. . . ."

"Directly. . . ."

"And murdered him in the most savage way imaginable."

"It was a fair exchange," said Gillis, fixing his clear blue eyes on me for the first time. "He'd stolen my confidence."

Kneesocks

*"Dear Harry," the letter began. "You probably don't remember
me, but I thought I'd take a chance and write – in the hope that
you would. We knew each other in The Long Ago and dated for
several months. (My name was Sybil Barnard at the time.) Then
we drifted apart. Since that time, I've been married, had two
sets of twins and have recently gotten divorced.* ☺/☹ *I have
followed your career with a great deal of interest – and thought
it might be fun to get together – and catch up on old times. I'll be
at the Plaza Hotel Nov. 7,8, visiting my sister, and wonder if
you would consider meeting me for a drink. I certainly hope so.
If not – I wish you continued good luck – and just write this off
as the idle fantasy of an (ex) suburban housewife. . . .*

> *Fondly,*
> *Sybil Barnard Michaels*

HARRY REMEMBERED HER, of course. How could he not remember her? He had thought about her for the last twenty-five
years, if not every day, then at least once a week for sure. She was
The One Who Got Away. Or, more correctly, The One Who Broke
His Heart And Got Away. She had been a drama student at the
University of Colorado; Harry reviewed the plays she was in for
the local newspaper. He had dated her in his senior year. She was
tall and blonde and beautiful in a quite regal way, and although
Harry was in love with her, they had never slept together, which
may have been why she broke off their romance so suddenly, and
in Harry's view, with such brutality. Their dates consisted for the
most part of the two of them dancing together, along with other

157

couples, in the parlor room of Harry's boarding house. At some point in the evening, her skin would become damp and she would start to quiver.

"Take me home when I feel like this," she would say.

And Harry would dutifully and gallantly whip her right back to her sorority house. Whenever they passed the wooded area, where couples slipped off to be together in total privacy, she would say: "Whatever you do, don't take me in there." And Harry would assure her that he had no intention of doing so. They continued along this way, taking walks, seeing an occasional movie together and dancing – less and less dreamily as time went by – in Harry's boarding house parlor. One night, her hand brushed against his erection and she jumped and Harry apologized and told her not to worry, it would never happen again.

In some section of himself, Harry had the sense that all they were doing was treading water. He liked being with Sybil, liked the *idea* of her, but he didn't really know what he was supposed to do next. One night, she asked: "You wouldn't ever consider meeting me in Denver and taking a hotel room, would you?" Harry said of course he wouldn't. This time even Harry knew what she was driving at – but he was twenty years old and had never rented a hotel room before. The thought of walking through the lobby with Sybil and dealing with the desk clerk was more than he could handle. Maybe if she had phrased it differently – or if *she* had arranged for the room.

One night, Harry returned to the boarding house after a film course in which the class had dissected "The Loves of Gosta Berling." Waiting for him at the top of the stairs was his roommate Travis, who was smiling broadly.

"You have a call," said Travis, who must have known what was in store for Harry and was enjoying the moment immensely. He accompanied Harry to the wall booth, as if he were a *maitre d'* and stood by smartly as Harry picked up the receiver. Sybil was at the other end and wasted no time in telling Harry that she didn't want to see him anymore.

"I didn't come all the way out here to date just one person."

Harry pleaded with her to give him another chance, but she wouldn't budge.

"Maybe after we graduate . . . if you're ever in Charlotte," she said. "But not now."

Harry was sick to his stomach after he hung up, which did not deter Travis from telling him – again, with enormous pleasure – that Sybil had been dating an agriculture major on the nights when she wasn't seeing him. Oddly enough, Harry did not hold any of this against Travis. His friend, who was the school's only male cheerleader, had suffered a series of romantic setbacks of his own, all with girls named Mary, and obviously took comfort in having some company.

Harry didn't give up. The next night, he caught up with Sybil, who was on her way to rehearsals for *The Wild Duck*, and begged her to go out with him one more time.

"I have something to show you," he said, suggestively, "that I've never shown you before."

She reacted to this with a little smile, indicating to Harry that the agriculture major had shown her all she needed to see. He trailed her across the campus, asking her if he could at least have a picture of her for his wallet, but she said she didn't think it would be a good idea.

"Not even a *picture*?" he said, as she disappeared into the rehearsal hall. That seemed awfully cruel to him; spitefully, he made no mention of her in his favorable review of *The Wild Duck*.

He didn't eat or sleep in the weeks that followed. To Travis's great delight, Harry could not even get fried chicken past his throat – the ultimate test of romantic misery. The other fellows in the boarding house, Travis excepted, gave him lots of room and lowered their voices sympathetically whenever he walked by. One night, Harry ran into Sybil's roommate, who looked him over quizzically and said: "You're such a nice man," which really pissed him off.

Soon afterward, Harry recovered slightly and took up with another drama student – from Wisconsin – who slapped her hips against his on their first date and led *him* into the woods. They made love virtually around the clock, in deserted classrooms, in the library, in the woods. One result was that Harry came up with the worst case of poison ivy in the history of the school and had to just lie there in the hospital under a sheet for days at a time. But none of this erased the memory of Sybil.

Harry saw her only one more time, dancing with the agriculture major at the Senior Prom, her face close to his and her fingers on his neck. Harry was with the Wisconsin drama student, who looked great and was extremely jolly – but it didn't help, and he spent the evening with his heart in his shoes.

After he graduated, and in the years that followed, Harry continued to nurse the memory of his loss, like an old football injury. It's entirely possible that he got married because of Sally's fairly close resemblance to his first love. Maybe there was more to it, but he didn't think so. So you could argue that Harry had to endure an entire unnecessary marriage and have a child and then get a divorce – all because of Sybil. And she wanted to know if he remembered her.

Strangely enough – and call it ego if you will – Harry had always known that he would hear from Sybil. And maybe even get a letter from her, similar to the one he held in his hand. Each time Harry received a credit on a movie, or even a partial, he wondered if she had seen his name on the screen. She was out there somewhere; surely she went to the movies. He didn't see how she could possibly have missed his name entirely, particularly in the case of his Two Big Pictures.

When she saw his name up there, Harry wondered if she had ever regretted her decision to dump him unceremoniously without so much as a farewell photograph.

Now that he had the letter, he could hardly wait for Julie to get back from the construction site so he could tell her about it. The great thing about Julie was that he could tell her about an episode like this with no fear of criticism. And he could count on her to enjoy it along with him. They had been living together at the beach for two years now, a couple of hours' drive from the city. Julie was working for the Post Office when they met and had made a recent switch over to carpentry, which she enjoyed more than delivering the mail. Each morning, she went off to join her construction crew – a great bunch of guys from Greenport – while Harry stayed behind and worked on the screenplay he was doing for a little Czech company that paid him in cash. He was enormously proud of Julie for going into carpentry. And the look of her in work clothes was a tremendous turn-on. One day, he had run into her accidentally at the deli, reading off sandwich orders for the crew from a two-by-four and he had wanted to pull off her blue jeans right on the spot.

When Julie got home around five, Harry said he had something to tell her and she said great, but could he hold on for a minute while she settled in. He said fine and did his best to bide his time while she went to the john, checked the mail and popped open an Amstel Light. Then she lit a Nat Sherman cigaretello and plopped down in a living room chair, with one leg slung over the armrest and told him to fire away. She did not like to listen to Harry's stories on the fly. Or at least his new ones.

Harry told her about Sybil and the letter and didn't she think he ought to meet her at the Plaza and play it out. Julie didn't agree wholeheartedly, but she did agree a little bit and said that if Harry wanted to meet her he should go ahead and do so. Instead of letting it rest, Harry said it would give the experience some closure, a new term he had picked up from the psychiatrist he had been seeing on and off for several years. Julie said she understood the concept and could see that it would be important for him to have some closure.

"But what if she's gorgeous?" she asked.

Harry had never seen anyone with eyes like Julie's. They could be warm and playful and kind, all at the same time. That, and the work boots and the carpentry. Sometimes it was too much for him.

"It's beside the point," said Harry. "This was twenty-five years ago."

"I don't care," said Julie. "And what if she sees your shoulders and tush?"

Harry said she had already seen them and decided he had to have Julie.

"Now?" she said, in mock panic. "When I haven't read the *Post*? And I haven't come down from my carpentry?"

"Right now."

"Okay," she said, with a sigh and took off her sweatshirt. "But let's not get into a whole big thing."

Harry was understandably jumpy on the day he was scheduled to meet Sybil. Normally, on his trips to the city, he stayed over at a hotel, since he didn't relish the idea of driving back and forth in one day. But on this occasion, he made sure not to book a room, probably as a safeguard against things getting out of hand. There was another reason Harry was edgy. He feared that he would see a record of his own aging in Sybil's face.

As he walked through the lobby of the hotel, Harry wondered if he would be able to recognize Sybil. He had reserved a table in a dark corner of *Trader Vic's*, just in case she had gotten fat. Call him a swine if you like, but he was not anxious to be caught having lunch with a fat, older woman. There were several middle-aged women in the lobby who were clearly not her. After fifteen minutes of looking around, Harry started to get irritated and wondered if she had changed her mind and decided not to show up at all. That would put him in the position of having to think about her for another twenty-five years. With no closure. And then she walked up to him – or marched up to him, more accurately – and Harry literally received the shock of his life. She was all furs and pearls and white skin and fragrance, and she was far more beautiful than Julie – or Harry, for that matter – had feared.

"Hi," she said, kissing him on the cheek. "Sorry, I'm late."

"That's perfectly all right," said Harry, who was every bit as unsettled as he had been the first time he met her at the sorority house and helped her on with her coat. His choice of *Trader Vic's* had turned out to be a good one, he felt, but for another reason. He wanted to be alone with her in the dark setting.

He led her off to the restaurant. After they had settled into the corner booth and ordered Mai Tais, she said he looked exactly the same.

"Maybe a little less hair," she said, after another quick study.

Harry raised one hand to his forehead and felt it was a fair appraisal. Actually, he thought he had gotten off easy.

"And you look fabulous," he said, deciding, in his new maturity, not to add that she hadn't aged a day. It was best, he felt, to leave out age altogether.

"I couldn't figure out what to wear," she said. "I thought maybe kneesocks."

"Kneesocks," he said, reverentially.

The thought of her long slender legs in kneesocks made him dizzy. He wanted to run right off with her and have her put some on for him.

He said it again.

"Kneesocks."

She brought him up to date on her life – her marriage to an orthopedist, the divorce, the two sets of twins, and the humdrum suburban life which was obviously no match for what she perceived as Harry's exciting one. She said the main reason she had come to the city was to see if she could find work in the theatre.

"I thought possibly you could help me."

"What kinds of parts would you play?" he asked.

Her face fell and Harry saw that she had taken it the wrong way – or maybe the right way – and he wished he could have taken back the question. As it was, he made a limp effort to paper it over.

"Now that I think about it," he said, "there are all *kinds* of roles you could handle."

She took a little time to recover, but once they were back on track he quickly worked Julie into the conversation, saying they were great friends and had been living together for two years at the beach.

"She's a carpenter," said Harry.

The fact that he and Julie were great friends and that she was a carpenter did not seem to make much of an impression on Sybil.

"I'm so delighted you remembered me," she said.

Harry was happy to admit that not only did he remember her but that she had rarely been out of his thoughts. And then he couldn't resist reminding her of the sudden and seemingly cruel way in which she had dropped him, without so much as a farewell photograph.

"I *hated* my photograph," she said. "Surely you didn't expect me to give you a photograph I hated."

Then she lowered her eyes.

"And I was afraid of you then. You were so sophisticated."

All of this was news to Harry. The photograph explanation made sense, but the thought of Harry being sophisticated at twenty – and of someone being afraid of him – was laughable. He wasn't sure how sophisticated he was right that minute.

"I wasn't ready for you then," she added, leaving the impression – unless Harry was way off the mark again – that she just might be ready for him now.

To shore up his man-of-the-world credentials, Harry stretched back and said he had done just about everything. She matched him in the erotic department by saying she had done just about everything herself. Then she cocked her head and thought for a second, as if to set the record straight.

"Except for two things."

Harry didn't inquire as to what they were. Why take the risk of having the reunion come to a crashing halt. But he certainly did wonder what the two things were. He guessed that one of them had to do with the backdoor route. As to the second, he didn't have a clue.

"I guess I've been waiting for the right time to do them," she added.

Harry couldn't handle that one at all, so he let it sit there for awhile. Then she asked if he was free for dinner. She was meeting her sister and brother-in-law, who was a therapist. The plan was for them to attend a party in Queens for a woman who was dying. Friends and relatives had been invited to sit around with her, in a party atmosphere, with incense burning, while she continued to die.

"It's kind of a die-in, I suppose," she said. "Would you like to come along? Afterward, we have a reservation at a Thai restaurant."

Harry said that under normal circumstances, he would love to join her, but he had promised Julie he'd be home in time for dinner.

She pressed him on it, but he held his ground. And then he paid the check and walked her to the elevator which took a long time to get there. While they were waiting, she tilted her head up to be kissed, in the sorority style, and Harry took her up on it, not quite getting all of her mouth, no doubt because he was torn twenty different ways. But he felt the length of her, the long legs, and the spare chest. Then his hands dropped to the substantial, maybe oversubstantial bottom that didn't quite go with the rest of it – and he saw for the first time that it wasn't his youth and inexperience and fear that had kept him from taking her into the woods many years back. The fit wasn't quite right, and it wasn't quite right now. He had probably known it then too, but had preferred to blank it out so that he could hold on to the sweet agony he felt in the years that followed. Still, he enjoyed her fragrance, the freshness of her mouth, the rich feel of her fur coat against his cheek. Harry had been leading a quiet, pleasant life, but there had been something missing, and now he thought he knew what it was.

"Would you like to come up for a drink?" she asked.

He looked at his watch and said he'd love to, but that he had better not.

"I have to get moving if I want to miss the rush hour."

"Well," she said, clearly disappointed, "if you ever get to Charlotte . . ."

Charlotte again. Twenty-five years later. He thought about the house and the twins and the way she lived, but he knew he was never going to see any of it. All the same, he told her that if he was ever in the area of Charlotte, he would be sure to look her up.

They shook hands, and with her fragrance still trailing after him, Harry headed straight to the gift shop. Because of the kiss, he felt he had better pick up something for Julie. He had been struggling with a film project that had to do with wood nymphs and, as luck would have it, he found a vanity table mirror that had a wood nymph for a handle. Harry picked it up and was about to bring it over to the sales clerk when he spotted a gossip columnist he knew at the magazine rack. He was all filled up with his recent experience and decided to tell the gossip columnist about it, even though he didn't know her very well.

"You'll never guess what just happened," he said.

And then it all came pouring out in a rush, starting with the college romance and his broken heart, the passage of time and then, years later, the letter, all of it culminating in the lunch he'd just had at *Trader Vic's*. She listened without comment and when he had finished, she pointed to the mirror and said: "That is the tackiest piece of shit I have ever seen."

There was still some daylight remaining when he got home. He went straight up to the bedroom and found Julie curled up on the bed, with a lapful of mysteries, puffing on a Nat Sherman cigaretello and working her way through a six-pack of Amstel Lights. In other words, all of her favorite things to do. He wondered how one person could read so many mysteries until one day he caught her skipping ahead and unconscionably peeking at the last page of one.

"So how'd it go, stud?" she asked, not quite taking her eyes off the book she was working on.

"Just fine," he said.

The casual tone made her look up.

"What do you mean by that?"

"What I said," he answered, slinging his coat on top of the jumble of clothing piled up on a chair. "It went just fine."

Harry gave her the gift and when she had unwrapped it she said it was very nice. The lack of enthusiasm didn't bother Harry. It took her awhile to warm up to gifts. In another month or so, she would go around saying it was one of the best things she owned.

"Was she gorgeous?"

"In a way," said Harry, popping open one of her precious Amstels.

"In what way was that?" she asked, her interest picking up. And then, with a playful kind of panic, she said: "You didn't *do* anything, did you?"

"How can you ask a question like that?" he said, continuing the game.

And then, before she could get out another one of her *Harry's*, with her eyes dancing, he sunk down beside her in the unmade bed in a tangle of beers and mysteries and laundry and cigarettes and blue jeans that was his life whether he liked it or not and hugged her so hard he almost broke her bones. He knew then that he loved her upside down and inside out, fat or skinny, rich or poor, sick, healthy, the whole list. He loved her wet green eyes, the chuckle, her rough hands, the right one extended, palm up, when she wanted to make a serious point. He loved her whiskey voice, her teenage breasts, her crazy hair, after a shampoo and before one, too, and if she didn't want to be buried right next to him, he would be disappointed, but that would be all right, too, as long as she gave it some serious thought. He wanted her, and if he didn't know it the instant he met her, he knew it ten minutes later. *Her.* The very word made him weak.

He just wished she'd wear a skirt once in awhile.

The People Person

THE BLINDFOLD had been removed. His abductors had left the room. To clear his head and adjust his eyes to the lighting took thirteen minutes. He was effective at this kind of calculation. He was tied, in a sitting position, to a rattan chair, which seemed odd, since he could move himself about – and the chair as well – if he chose to. But there seemed no point to it, so he decided to stay put, at least for the time being. The room was cheaply, but cheerfully, decorated. There were two other rattan chairs that were dime store versions of the furniture he had back at the ranch. There were also twin beds, and an overhead television set with a blank screen, positioned at an odd angle. You would have to twist your head around to watch it. There was a kitchenette and a microwave, but no stove. He guessed the small dining area led to a bathroom that he could not see.

Irony was not his strong suit, but it struck him as being ironic that the most powerful man in the world was tied helplessly to a chair in what appeared to be a small studio apartment.

The flat was painted in hot tropical colors as were several tourist-style paintings of parrots that hung on one wall. There was something familiar about the setting. The flowered sheets, he soon realized, reminded him of a bordello that he had visited half a dozen times as a young man. It was situated on the Texas/Mexico border.

He had tried mightily to keep his youthful transgressions out of the campaign. Still, hints about drugs and wild women kept leaking out. He had told the press that as a young man, he had been somewhat "carefree." As far as he was concerned, that statement ended the discussion and the press appeared to be satisfied.

But the flowered bed sheets brought back the memory of his gaud-
ier days. In his new set of beliefs, he had begun to regard the bordello visits as being "sinful." But he could not deny that they had
been among the most pleasurable days of his youth. There was one
cheerful woman in particular. An excellent storyteller and a gifted
practitioner, she combined both skills during their hours together.
From time to time – when he needed some erotic assistance – he
thought of her. He wished her well, and hoped she had ended up
in a good place.

He thought back to the actual abduction and had to concede
that it had been pulled off with great precision. He had paid a state
visit to a small energy-rich Latin American country, one that he
was anxious to "win over" with the loopy charm that even his
adversaries conceded was an effective political weapon. The security warnings were clear and emphatic, even ominous. The country, which was benign on the surface, had the potential of turning
instantly into a tinderbox. He was instructed not to make contact
with the crowds, however adoring they might appear to be. Yet for
a moment, at the airport, he could not resist reaching out to
embrace several of his more ardent admirers. The phrase "people
person" nauseated several of his more sophisticated aides, but he
felt it fit him perfectly. And this capability – his complete ease
around the masses – had served him well in his swift political rise.
Thus, feeling surrounded by love, he had left his protective cordon
for what seemed like an instant. And as he did so, an almost math-
ematically precise seam had opened in the crowd, as if it had been
created by a laser. He found himself being drawn through this passage with all the ease of a sword being removed from a scabbard.
There were some casualties. He had a hazy recollection of gunfire
and bodies on the ground. One was that of a favorite of his – a
square-jawed and tow-headed "true believer" who reminded him
of his nephew. He got a blurred and tumultuous look at his
masked abductors. For all of their efficiency, they were a ragtag
bunch. Their uniforms did not match. Some were all in black, others in faded denim. The man who might have been their leader

was older than the others. A graying and out-of-date ponytail hung slackly at the back of his neck. There was an expanse of white flesh showing at his less than trim waistline. Was he an old rocker? Though his face was concealed, he had the look of a man who had failed in many professions.

Unsurprisingly, each of the abductors carried a Kalishnikov rifle. Two, or perhaps three, were women. They were slender and fit, much more so than their male counterparts. He wondered what it would be like to make love to one of them – though he realized that as a Believer, the very thought was not permissible. As he struggled to suppress the sinful fantasy, he was rushed into the back seat of old Cadillac; it had a musty smell and might have belonged to an impoverished grad student. He was blindfolded, forcefully and expertly, by one of the female abductors. Then he felt the sting in his right arm. He heard a voice say "Goodnight, Prexy." And then he settled into a comatose state that was not unpleasant. He had no idea how far they had traveled and whether they had remained in the vehicle for the trip. He remembered only that he had been in the back seat of the car and that he had awakened in a spotless studio apartment.

One of the female abductors fed him bites of a burrito which strengthened his feeling that he was in a tropical area. It was surprisingly tasty, though not on the list of acceptable foods that had been prescribed for his acid reflux attacks. When he'd finished the burrito, a Diet Pepsi (also not on his list) was raised to his lips. The gentle manner of his abductor led him to believe that he was not going to be tortured – at least in the conventional manner. Was it possible his abductor was wearing perfume? And if so, did he recognize the scent? She dabbed at his face with a napkin, then said goodbye with a pat on his knee and turned out the lights. He regretted that he was not in a position to appoint her to something.

He had a difficult time for the next hour. All he could hear was the shuffling of footsteps in the corridor and some grunting, as if crates of some kind were being carried or shoved along. His prominent nose, which had been the butt of editorial jokes, began to itch and of course he had no way of scratching it. Crying out "Please scratch my nose" was not an acceptable option. Abandoned now and facing an unknown fate, he decided to call upon his Maker. Call he did, but there was no discernible response. This disappointed him since he'd been assured that there would always be help of some kind from above.

Though occasionally short-tempered, he was basically optimistic. Yet he began to feel that there would be no happy resolution to his predicament. He was, at heart, a trader and a businessman. In his current state, he had nothing to exchange for his freedom.

The lights came on with a sudden and almost painful intensity. Each of his abductors carried in a cardboard carton, struggling with the weight of it. They set down the cartons, then paused to take a breath. The cartons were then unpacked. Each contained books. The handsomely embossed bindings suggested that they were classics. He had noticed such volumes in the Executive Library. Once, in an idle moment, he had even taken one down from the shelves, thinking it might contain salacious passages. When he found little along this line, he replaced the book and paid no further attention to the shelves.

Squatting, the lead abductor with the awful ponytail selected one of the volumes, opened it and pointed to the opening paragraph.

The captive looked out at the piles of books that were set out before him. By rough count, there must have been five hundred volumes. He felt a rising sense of panic.

"All of them?" he asked, in a strangled voice.

"Every bloody one," said the leader.

For the first time, guns were pointed seriously in his direction. Though his throat was dry, his eyes watered. Once they had focused, he began to read.

"Happy families are all alike; every unhappy family is unhappy in its own way."

The Great
Beau LeVyne

A NOVELLA

YEARS BACK, and just before I met Beau, I thought my life had come to an end. I'd found out from a friend that my wife – who had been my college sweetheart – was having an affair with a musician. There are marriages that can survive an affair – or even flourish in the teeth of one if you believe the popular magazines – but ours was not one of them. The friend – acting out of either malice or good intentions – told me about my wife and her lover during a performance of The Doors at a club on Manhattan's West 46th Street. I knew that what she told me was true. Though technically it dragged on for a bit, the marriage ended effectively with the delivery of this news. I had written a first play that was running in the Village at the time, but the triumph had no savour and I felt useless and without hope. And then, suddenly and thrillingly, I found myself flying along the Long Island Expressway in a sky blue convertible with two new friends at my side – Beau LeVyne and Jane Sandler – and the feeling that there were fresh new possibilities ahead.

Beau had seen and admired the play and called to arrange for me to meet a group of producers and agents with the idea of my doing a screenplay for a film version. I had no special interest in film at the time, but since I had nothing better to do, I agreed to meet Beau and his group at the *Italian Pavilion* in mid-town Manhattan. When I arrived at the restaurant, my attention was drawn

173

to a powerfully built man who seemed barely able to have crowded himself into his well-cut pinstriped suit. He had a rich suntan, a fairly prominent nose and kept his sparse sandy-colored hair plastered back unashamedly in the matador style. I can't say that he was handsome, but he carried himself with assurance and behaved as if he were. He circled the room, greeting people at the table and at the bar. I thought at first he might be the maître d'. He turned out to be Beau LeVyne.

For whatever reason, he recognized me and introduced himself. I found him immediately to be open-mannered and to have a boyish sweetness about him. He seemed genuinely pleased to meet me; on the spot, we entered seamlessly into a friendship that was to last twenty-five years. Actually, it felt more as if we were resuming a friendship rather than starting one.

"I can't tell you how much these people love you, Cliff," he said, as he led me to the table he had reserved.

The luncheon meeting passed quickly. There was some give and take on the approach to the proposed film. But when the subject was broached as to who would actually pay for the work, there was a general clearing of throats, some uneasy shuffling and the meeting dribbled away into nothing. When the other participants had filed out, Beau shook his head sadly and said: "Can you *believe* these people, Cliff?" as if he'd had nothing to do with assembling them.

Despite this unpromising start, we saw each other several times over the course of the next few weeks. He was on good and familiar terms with a great many artists, sports figures and writers in particular, but it was difficult to pin down what Beau himself actually *did*. It wasn't that he was unemployed. At the moment, he was working as the personal assistant to a prominent figure in the recording industry, but his responsibilities were vague. Since he was available to meet me, no matter what the time of day or night, I had to wonder if he ever showed up at his office. He had attended Princeton – for one semester as it turned out – and had a background as an athlete, although here, too, the details were murky.

An injury had supposedly cut short his career. Indeed, he shuffled along rather than walked; when he stood still, his toes pointed inward as if he were forever standing at a free throw line. The second time we met, he presented me with a photograph of himself, dressed as a matador and fighting a bull in Spain. The inscription read:

"To Cliff . . . My new best friend . . . With admiration . . . Beau."

The photograph was impressive, although, as I pointed out uncharitably, when I showed it to others, the bull was no bigger than my Labrador Retriever.

Beau asked me to read a short story of his. I thought it was polished and professional, though it remained a puzzle, since it was the only story he was ever known to have written. It was published in an obscure literary quarterly. He was tremendously comfortable to be with and would ride along agreeably in any conversational direction, registering a slight demurral now and then ("How can you *say* that, Cliff?") but then falling quickly back into line, no matter what the thrust of the argument. ("That's *always* been my feeling, Cliff. Surely you know that.") On only one occasion do I recall him taking a stiff position and refusing to budge from it. The novelist Irwin Shaw, in an interview, had said that his stories were a form of letter home, a means of telling friends where he was, what he was thinking and what he was up to. I said this made sense to me. But the whole idea of it outraged Beau.

"It's drivel, Cliff," he said. "You can't possibly agree with him."

It was as if he had to have one firm position of his own – or perhaps he thought of writing as a higher calling than I did.

Despite his generally pliable style, or possibly because of it, I was a little afraid of him.

One night, he called to invite me to a cast party on Eastern Long Island in celebration of the completion of *Lilith,* a film to which he had some mysterious connection. I decided to ask along Jane Sandler, a young schoolteacher I had met at a pottery class of all

places. (I was out of control, flailing around idiotically for something to do.) She had taught me how to make love slowly and
exquisitely – and probably how to make love at all. She had soft
brown eyes, a comforting voice – and I'm afraid I lack the ingenu-
ity to describe her without making reference to her breasts, which
were magnificent. Years later, at the steak house on Morris Island
where we met frequently, Beau would look off in the distance,
lower his voice reverentially and say; "I still cannot *believe* Jane
Sandler's tits."

I picked her up in the sports car I had bought with the first royalties from my play – and probably as a consolation prize for losing
my wife. Beau joined us and then there we were, speeding along in
the cool and promising air of Eastern Long Island. We had little difficulty in being admitted to the set where Beau introduced us to
various of the principals. Jane slipped into the background and I
found myself dancing with Jean Seberg. I had seen her in "Breath-
less" and, along with half the country, had fallen in love with
her . . . or at least her performance. It was difficult for me to actually *see* her – she was all fairness and shimmer and international
fame; if someone had told me that I would once be holding this
apparition in my arms, I would have considered the notion absurd.

"You're Jean Seberg," I said, in my one attempt at speech.
"And I'm dancing with you."

When the music stopped, I released her, or rather broke away
in relief. I was not to see her again until years later when she
knocked on my door at midnight in the Beverly Hills Hotel and
asked me to buy a sewing machine for the wife of a black radical
living in Watts. As a spur, she produced a check from Sammy
Davis, Jr., whose room was further down the hall – and who had
already purchased one.

In the brief time we had been separated, Beau had developed a
mysterious grievance against Warren Beatty. With clenched fists
and a tight jaw, he led me to the star's trailer.

"Come on out, Warren," he shouted, pounding on the door. "I
know you're in there."

When there was no response, he put his shoulder against the door and tried to ram it down. I had seen that done by detectives in movies and always had an urge to try it. We took turns for awhile, the door finally collapsing on my watch, so to speak. The fact that it happened this way did not upset Beau so much as intrigue him.

"Cliff is stronger than I am," he would say, when introducing me to new friends; then he would look off as if consulting some distant source of knowledge, and add: "But I'm tougher."

A pretty young actress in a petticoat stood cowering in the corner of the trailer, holding one hand to her cheek, and with the other shielding herself with a dressing gown – yet another pose I had seen in films, possibly dating back to the silents. Crew members appeared and suddenly bodies were flying, with Beau and me standing literally back-to-back, punching out at flesh and furniture. It was completely impersonal and tremendously exhilarating – something else I'd always longed to do. Never once did it occur to me that I or someone else might end up blinded or otherwise maimed for life. Police sirens sounded in the distance. When I pulled myself out of the rubble, I was miraculously intact, and anxious to have another try at it. It was as if I'd survived a wild ride in an amusement park. I felt a slight tug of reality when the police actually arrived. The fact that they were *state* troopers, with their no-nonsense reputation – was unnerving. A set designer, holding a limp arm, pointed us out as the instigators. Then Beau, in a fine moment, brushed himself off and with a disbelieving shake of his head, said to one of the troopers, "I cannot believe you can go through four years as a Marine and then have something like *this* happen."

The trooper nodded sympathetically. Before I knew it, we had scooped up Jane and were back in the car, racing along the highway, reviewing the adventure, embroidering it – all of which was as much fun as the episode itself. Then, as we neared the city, and the whiskey began to wear off, I realized that I was having a private celebration. Though they sat beside me, Jane and Beau were in a world of their own, speaking intensely as if they had just met on a first date. Where did she live? What books did she like? *The Stranger?* Beau *loved* The *Stranger.* Could they meet for drinks the following night? She didn't see why not. This time *I* was the one who could not believe what was happening. Beau and I took turns doing things that the other couldn't believe. I said nothing, as if I was impervious to it all. To comment would have shown that I lacked sophistication, which was unthinkable. But didn't he know what I was going through, how torn up I was at the time? He had his wife and daughters, I had only Jane – and yet here he was, casually taking her away from me. What was going through *Jane's* mind, for that matter, although it didn't occur to me at the time that she had any part in it.

I dropped them off at separate addresses and began to feel shabby about the evening. The set designer, who became prominent, never forgave me. Whenever we met, he would take on a grim look and go into a defensive crouch, as if preparing to fend off an attack. I tried to dismiss the *Lilith* episode as hijinks – maybe Beau was a fighter . . . I certainly wasn't . . . but the set designer wasn't having any.

"Oh, sure," he would say to his wife. "Cliff holds 'em and Beau hits 'em."

As it turned out, Beau didn't quite have his wife, Heidi, after all. I met them together at a book party some months later, one of the many gatherings to which he had easy and unquestioned access. I was no longer seeing Jane. Our sad little romance, more of a convalescence for me actually, continued with a series of desperate little hand-holding encounters at Irish bars in midtown, and then petered out entirely. I had asked her about her date with Beau. She would say only that they had taken a long walk and that he had behaved like a gentleman. This disappointed me since I'd been expecting, and possibly hoping for something that had more bite to it. And I sensed that she was not telling me the entire story.

Beau sat alone at the party in an almost visible black cloud.

The effect was off-putting. One of the guests was a critic named McMartin who had known Beau for several years. I learned from him that Beau's sister had committed suicide.

"She leapt from a boat in Caracas to which she'd fled to join her married lover."

Though barely out of Wellesley, according to McMartin, she had been married twice and lived for a time in Pakistan. Through some curious inversion of logic, I found this troubled and frantic background to be romantic. The good schools, the fact that she was Beau's sister, the impulsive behavior – I was convinced that had we met I would have been in love with her.

Though Beau said little, he was stretched out elaborately on a divan in the center of the room. There was something flamboyant about his grief. This shifted the focus of the party away from the short story writer whose work was being celebrated and who began to flounce about in irritation.

"Forgive me," he said to McMartin, with a nod in Beau's direction, "but who exactly *is* this person?"

From time to time, guests, myself included, would wander over to Beau, pat him sympathetically on the shoulder and otherwise try to console him. A major novelist sat beside him and told him in a whisper of a loss that he himself had suffered in Paris, all of which failed to penetrate the gloom. McMartin said to me: "He's been carrying on like this in public for weeks."

I introduced myself to Heidi who stood apart from Beau at the party. She was a slender raven-haired woman with exquisite skin and patrician features whose flesh was cold to the touch. As I was later to learn, she had been a Homecoming Queen at the University of Missouri, majored in political science and then veered off to become a curator at the Indian Museum. She now spoke with an English accent that was convincing. The two had met at a resort in Barbados and must have made a striking couple. They still did, though they had little to do with one another at the party. Though we hadn't met before, she said I had been pointed out to her at the theatre one night.

"I was struck by the care and concern you showed for your wife, Cliff."

Evidently I'd been held up in the LeVyne household as an example of good domestic behavior. A lot of good it did me, I thought.

As the party proceeded, Beau, from time to time, would call out to his wife: "Hey, cunt, let's go home," a remark the other guests chose not to hear and which Heidi threw off with a nervous chuckle. Despite this display, which went beyond rudeness, I continued to be envious of anyone whose family was intact. Was there a lesson in this, I wondered. Treat a wife with civility and lose her. Call her a cunt in public and she's yours forever.

Heidi left without him. Later on, I joined Beau and a small group in a funereal walk back to his brownstone in Brooklyn Heights. One member of our group was a film animator who listened to Beau's mournful lament and then cut him off sharply.

"Stop feeling sorry for yourself," he said. "You're behaving like an idiot."

He was a thin, hollow-chested man who wore thick glasses and whose animated characters were as pathetic-looking as he was. I wondered what I could do to keep Beau from attacking him. Indeed, Beau rose up murderously and narrowed his eyes in a look I was to see many times again. But then he withdrew cheerfully, invited us all up for a drink and was never heard to mention his loss again.

Beau turned up next at a literary symposium that was held at a university in South Carolina; there wasn't a clue as to what he was doing there and why he was invited or if he had indeed been invited at all. Writers in various disciplines had been given $1000 each by a foundation to show up for several days and to discuss The Novelist as Journalist or The Journalist as Novelist – or some other uncompelling topic. We were also expected to be available to the students. I flew down with McMartin. We were joined at a kick-off luncheon by Isaac Bashevis Singer who was the last to arrive and who had come by bus. After the first course had been served, the great novelist leaned across to me – I thought to impart some bit of philosophical wisdom.

"Do you mind, Mr. Adams," he said, "trading me your vegetables for my meat?"

A poet who had been in and out of institutions stood up and accused the group at large of being unsympathetic to the Palestinians. After he had pulled himself together, a novelist, with a shelf of lugubrious works to her credit, emphasized her seriousness of purpose to all who would listen.

"I'm not *funny*," she said, with a sharp glance in my direction.

"Neither is Cliff," said Beau, rallying to my defense.

The editor of a distinguished literary quarterly got up from the table, stretched wearily and said: "I can see this is another town in which I'm not going to get laid."

Beau did not participate in the main discussion – held in an auditorium – but walked about in some vague supervisory way, instructing sound technicians. Once again no one thought to question his function. We were all a bit strident on stage. I remember insisting, idiotically, that as a writer I needed to be situated at all times in the center of the action – whatever that meant. McMartin made an impassioned plea that he be allowed to work.

"I say to you one and all, my friends, *let me write*," he cried out to a puzzled audience which must have wondered, as I did, what was stopping him.

The atmosphere lightened up a bit toward evening when the poet's wife arrived to cart him off to a rest home, the strain of the events having proved too much for his fragile spirit. At a local restaurant, the novelist said she had seen a recent play of mine.

"It was an improvement over your earlier one."

She held forth for a bit on the low standard of American fiction after which the great Mr. Singer took me aside and said: "Tell me, Mr. Adams, why does she wear such little skirts?"

A group of locals became abusive, hollering out catcalls in our direction. Taking courage from the presence of Beau, who sat beside him, the quarterly editor proposed that we fight them, a suggestion that received little support from the group.

"Do they know about my arms?" Beau asked, with a look in the direction of the offending group. Actually, his arms were of modest size, the great strength coming up from his trunk. The locals quieted down, and it's possible the sight of his brooding and menacing figure had much to do with it.

After dinner, Beau and the novelist went for a walk on the campus. Several hours later, he returned, in an exasperated state, to the dormitory in which we were housed.

"I have never met anyone that horny in my *life*," he said, collapsing into a chair.

"Did you fuck her?" asked the quarterly editor cheerfully.

"Did I fuck her," Beau repeated with derision.

"Well, did you?" the editor persisted.

"Cliff," Beau appealed to me, "Can you believe he asked me that?"

The question went unanswered, Beau not deigning to answer it specifically.

We gathered the next morning for breakfast and then went off to our final responsibility which was to speak informally to students in the class to which we had been assigned. Beau disappeared down one of the corridors and I still have no idea of where he went. He had no assignment. Did he visit a class all the same? If so, who did he say he was and what did he talk about? Or did he pretend to visit some phantom class and continue to pace the corridors? What had he told his employer to explain his mid-week absence? What was his reason for making the trip, which all seemed so unnecessary and sad?

Beau owned a cottage on what I think of as a dark and cruel stretch of beach at the northern tip of Morris Island. Built of rough stone, it seemed more of a lair than a home. He went about and virtually lived in a loincloth made of black lycra that was ill-suited to his thick body. Mike Tyson, the heavyweight fighter who was built along similar lines, was later to popularize the style. Each morning, at dawn, Beau would invade the ocean and swim out for miles. I rented a cottage nearby. Although I was much too respectful of the strong undertow to join him – frightened actually – I did watch Beau several times. Predictably, he was a powerful swimmer. But it was as if he swam not so much for pleasure as to match his strength against the tide. He did much the same with Danny, the Labrador Retriever I brought along for company during the summer months. One morning, Beau came over for a visit and got down on a mat to wrestle with the animal. Playful at first, he began to mock the dog's mere eighty pounds of weight and to get the animal in a chokehold and to apply pressure. I had to talk Beau down quietly – I was always having to talk him down – and he gradually released his grip. But what if he had strangled my dog?

Though never quite content, he was as close to that state as he ever came during the summer months at the beach. He could feel that whatever race he was in had stalled – whatever phantom competitors he imagined had no doubt withdrawn for a few months, enabling him to do the same. Unshaven, charred by the sun, he holed up for most of the day, reading and rereading the novels of Ernest Hemingway until he had virtually memorized them, and generally attending to his family. From time to time, he would be seen in his loincloth, walking through a nearby gay community, in the style of a Western gunslinger invading a frontier town.

Each weekend, I took part in a fierce and often bloody volleyball game presided over by Beau and a Newport financier who made it clear that he disliked me. I'm a decent enough player, but I have an underhand serve and I tend to slap at the ball rather than lock my fingers and cradle it in the Olympic style that was coming into vogue at the time. It may be that the Newport man's feeling about me had only to do with my playing style although I doubt it. Our group was made up of stockbrokers, advertising executives, physicians and a celebrated actor who flung his tiny frame into the game and insisted that no special privileges be awarded his celebrity. There was an informal league along the beach, but our chief opponents were a houseful of hippies who played the game cheerfully and were unbegrudging about their almost automatic loss to us each weekend. They showed interest in the players' wives who came to watch the games, and as the summers rolled along, began romantically to pick them off one by one, luring the wives back to their commune. In some cases, the liaisons became permanent, with the result that the beach soon became denuded of stockbroker wives. An exception was Heidi, who received visits from a private school headmaster on days when Beau was away in Manhattan. Beau was aware of the man and dismissed him.

"I don't understand what she sees in that ridiculous faggot."

As marriages disintegrated, the games became vicious, with angry commodities men flying up in the air to spike the ball down on the heads of hippies who had broken up their families. One casualty was a plastic surgeon who broke three fingers on his operating hand and for six months was unable to correct noses.

Toward the end of one season, we were matched against a local industrial team for championship of the beach. With a crowd looking on, I took up my usual position and was asked by the Newport man to step aside.

"We're trying something else," he said, signaling to a boy who worked in the local supermarket to take my place.

I looked over at Beau who chuckled and pawed at the sand as if the affront was some minor inconvenience and could we please get on with the game. Humiliated, I watched from the sidelines and never played again. I said nothing to Beau, of course, since the vocabulary of our friendship did not have language for the expression of hurt feelings. Did he enjoy my pain? He had professed to care about me and would embarrass me in front of others by suddenly declaring: "I can't begin to tell you how much I love Cliff."

You can say that it was a meaningless game and that it certainly wasn't going to be reported in *Sports Illustrated* and that I should have been casual about the experience. Nonetheless, it stung.

I asked Margaret about Beau. She was a psychiatrist I was dating who was much older than me which had its own erotic appeal.

"He has a character flaw, darling," she said. "You won't find it in the textbooks."

She doled out such insights sparingly, roughly one each time we met, which fueled our brief affair and may have kept it going. I wondered how many she kept in reserve. Our brief affair ended when she insisted that we see each other three times a week – as if I were a patient. But she had wondered at the time why I kept up my friendship with Beau.

"It seems so unsatisfying."

I had no answer at the time. But I must have known, instinctively, that despite his bravado, the amatory and athletic achievements, both real and imagined, I could always count on Beau – no matter what my state – to be in worse shape than I was. I was not alone on this. Many of us took that strength from him. None of us realized the toll it was to take on him.

It will come as no surprise that we enjoyed going to the fights together. Beau arranged for our ringside tickets; I paid for them as I did for our dinners and nights on the town. I don't know if I had more money than he did, but he had the family and after my wife left me I had no interest in money. I spent whatever I earned in theatrical royalties as soon as I received it, almost as if it were an annoyance. We saw Roberto Duran, unknown then and sleek as a panther, defeat the lightweight champion Ken Buchanan and spit on him in the process. We watched Jose Torres literally paralyze Willie Pastrano with a single body blow, the latter never having been knocked down before.

My father was dying slowly from a blood disease, but he could still get around and on occasion, we took him along. My mother had died some years back and he lived alone in the apartment they had shared for many years in Stanford, Connecticut. I lacked the will and strength to have him come and live with me in one of the flats in Manhattan I rented every few years. Then, too, such an arrangement would have interfered with my rigid schedule of getting my work out of the way and trying to seduce as many women as possible – taking advantage of the glorious license that had been issued to one and all in the '70s: *Carry on to Your Heart's Content.*

I suppose the Fight Nights and an occasional dinner were a means of atoning for failing to care for my father in his last days. Beau told me that *his* father was a retired engineer who had spent many years abroad building dams. Mr. LeVyne joined us for one of the Fight Nights at Madison Square Garden. He was a small round-shouldered man who wore a fedora and a tan windbreaker and did not seem to fit the swashbuckling resume supplied by his son. Beau and his sister had been raised in a small flat on Eastern Parkway in Brooklyn. I kept wondering how Mr. LeVyne had been able to find the resources to send his children to Wellesley and Princeton. The two older men, both soft-spoken and roughly the same age, got along well. The Hispanic fighters were first coming into prominence at the time, and the new fans, from a more demonstrative culture, were more raucous than the usual mild-mannered Garden crowd. When a decision went against a Panamanian favorite, a hail of beer bottles rained down on us from the balcony. Using a bench as an overhead shield, both Beau and I led our respective fathers to safety.

We saw the first of the memorable Ali-Frazier fights. In the dressing room, Frazier, a man I had written about for a magazine, shook hands with my father and congratulated him on the iron grip, forged in New England textile mills, that this small courtly man was to maintain until he died. Afterward, we joined some boxing regulars at *Toots Shors* nearby. A promoter asked if I was satisfied with the complimentary tickets he had been giving to me and Beau.

"They were just fine," I said.

The news that the tickets were "comps" and that Beau had kept the money I'd given him to buy them was hardly devastating. I wasn't exactly out of pocket, since I thought all along I'd been paying for the tickets – but it was unsettling, one of the many little jolts in our friendship that I was to experience at regular intervals.

I have the uneasy feeling that I've been portraying myself as a monument of good behavior. It may be impossible to dig out from this posture, but I like to think that my transgressions – failing to care for a dying parent; suddenly, almost viciously shutting the door on an affair that no longer interested me – had more sweep to them than those of Beau.

Nor was I was an injured victim. No doubt, I upset my friend Beau as often as he did me. A cruel blow to him must have been my very existence – an unspoken but subtle (and smug?) reminder that as rudderless as my life had become I had at least some career achievement and he had none.

My circle of heroes shrinks as I get older, but I continue to be in sophomoric awe of outstanding writers and athletes, the latter posing a particular problem for me. What does one say to Pelé? Or Jerry Rice? What conversational opener is appropriate upon meeting Dominguin? Beau had no such inhibitions. On our nightly tours of the city's clubs and restaurants, he would disappear and then pop up at a table nearby, having an easy, bantering exchange with Reggie Jackson or Earl Monroe or whichever legend happened to be in the city. Somehow he would confer upon himself a status equal to theirs. After all, weren't he and Jim Brown, at bottom, both jocks, a pair of football greats out on the town? I believe he truly felt that he would have surpassed Brown in the record books were it not for the mysterious injury that cut short his athletic career at Princeton. And somehow, his relaxed style with them brought great heroes down to human proportions. At one of the small parties he gave at his immaculately-kept book-lined house in Brooklyn Heights, I met Kyle Rote who had always seemed Herculean on the football field. It came as a surprise that he was mortal after all, a man no taller than I am.

Beau read a great deal and for some unfathomable reason was on the mailing lists of publishers who sent him review copies of their latest novels. Whenever a notable first work of fiction appeared, Beau would somehow wind up with the author in tow, squiring the novelist about the city. He was on friendly if not intimate terms with established writers as well. Capote, Jones, Shaw, Algren, Mailer. Such men may have been Gods to me, but not to Beau who saw that they were plagued with indigestion, had to worry about money and divorce, and feared death. He was aware, as I was not, that the writing of *Lolita* did not encase Vladimir Nabokov permanently in a state of celestial bliss.

What did they see in him ? That he had charm was undeniable, although my friend Margaret – in one of her carefully parceled out insights – suggested that I examine this trait carefully. Do we really want to be charmed? By a charmer? In the company of distinguished writers he was neither self-consciously brash nor overly solicitous but would simply penetrate their celebrity without fear.

He didn't drink very much or smoke and the very smell of marijuana turned him sullen and listless. But there were times when the proximity of these substances got through to him and he would behave badly. One such night, at a restaurant, he challenged Bill Russell to a test of strength. He had to be held by the great NBA star at arms length – kicking in the air – until he calmed down. On another occasion he flexed in front of "Crazy Joe" Gallo, prompting the fabled mobster to get up from his dinner party and ask the restaurant proprietor ominously: "What do you want done with him?"

It was inevitable that he would match himself against the legendary "Pinhead," a bearded giant twice Beau's size, who had knocked out ranking heavyweights in saloons and was acknowledged to be the East Side's top bar fighter. McMartin stood by, puffing on his pipe, as the two wheeled round and round on a dark side street, Pinhead slamming Beau to the ground, picking him up to congratulate him ("You've got a lot of guts, kid") then flinging him against a tenement wall.

In his pinstriped suits and corporate ties, he was always fighting someone and he was gracious in defeat. One night he showed up late at *Elaine's* and cheerfully announced that he had just been knocked cold by the brother of a jewel thief in *K.C. Li's Restaurant* in the West Village. He would drop out of sight on occasion, then show up with fresh cuts and swollen cheekbones, alluding to a score he had had to settle in central Harlem.

One night, at a restaurant on Bleecker Street, a bedraggled poet came in from the street and sat down at our table. He recognized McMartin, had read a piece of his on Baudelaire and wanted to discuss it. When Beau asked him to leave, he refused.

"Now look," said Beau, puffing himself up. "Don't make me repeat myself."

The poet ignored him and decided to stay for dinner. The air went out of Beau who picked at his food morosely and said: "If there's anything I can't *stand*, it's someone who's above fighting."

In such situations, when confronted with someone of unprepossessing stature, but strong convictions, he generally backed off.

I had no reason to doubt his courage, but on reflection I can't think of a time when he actually came out on top in one of his many brawls. Which leads to the melancholy conclusion that actually *winning* fights was not on his agenda.

For an embarrassing number of years, and no doubt to the detriment of the magisterial plays I had planned to write, I was completely preoccupied with sex – hot, immediate, relentless, boundary-breaking, personal and anonymous, long-and-short-term, rough and gentle. I don't recall this being in a spirit of conquest, but I can't prove that it wasn't. More likely, it was designed to make up for some long period of deprivation in this area. I know it was a journey of some kind, through exquisite and for me unexplored terrain. Nor did I experience the hollow feeling that many insist must accompany such activity. It worked out nicely, and I got out, so to speak, when I was ahead.

Despite his unsettling last words – "There's nothing you can do for me" – my father left me some money, enough to buy but not furnish a small apartment in a midtown high-rise, which became a base for me. My territory, as it were, was a three-block area contiguous to my building. I focused on women who worked in the bank and the optometrist's shop on the ground floor – and in an upscale boutique I could see from my bedroom window. The advantages I had were that I was available and totally committed to the enterprise. Striving to avoid the mistake of my marriage, I generally chose situations in which I felt I had a slight advantage. Women who were attractive but not overly so. Women from the boroughs who had just discovered books and theatre. Others who were new arrivals from foreign countries. It's fair to say that I preyed on women, but also to point out that often as not I discovered that I was being preyed upon. This was particularly true of a disastrous affair I had with a woman from Ecuador. I thought I had ingeniously picked her up at a delicatessen – only to learn that she had researched my work at the library, was familiar with my brief entry in *Who's Who* – and had been sitting at the same table for several weeks in the hope that I would drop by.

Beau seemed to enjoy women, but was less relentless in his pursuit of them. His affairs had a rueful caste to them. When I think of him in this context he is sitting in the gloom of the Oak Bar of the Plaza Hotel at some defeated hour of the day, seeking comfort from a sturdy co-worker in tweeds. But there were more spirited times for him and I envied him several of the women he knew – a furiously attractive slip of an actress with an underbite and straw-colored hair who followed him about the city, trailing furs and money – and a dark-haired fashion model with a pornographic face who disappeared with him on a motorcycle one night and was never seen again.

He showed up at my door one afternoon with a huge Swedish woman in tow who spoke no English; with a finger to his lips, he cautioned me to be quiet, as if I were about to shout out something disruptive. Unnecessarily, she did cartwheels to be enticing, then undressed and lay back on the bed to receive us. We threw off our clothes swiftly and comedically. Unused to sharing women, I had trouble getting an erection. Beau, too, had his difficulties, the woman was unhelpful, and the two of us labored fruitlessly throughout the afternoon. At one point, in a tangle of flesh, he whispered: "Put it in my mouth." Lapsing idiotically into an English accent, I said: "I don't think so, old boy." It's important here to catch accurately the spirit of his offer, which was that of a soldier on a battlefield, offering to help out a wounded comrade. Or so I felt at the time. Glumly, we proceeded on our barren path . . . and then later, as we dressed forlornly in the darkness, Beau rescued the occasion with a single statement: "That woman can *never* claim she didn't get her pussy sucked."

There were the two houses, the cars, the school tuition, and for many years and through some sleight of hand, Beau managed to keep this precarious vessel afloat. He lasted an average of two years at his jobs; from the moment he was hired, it was as if he would set about to have himself fired – by slipping off to Morocco or Spain on trips that were only vaguely related to his work. In one case, while he was working at a supposedly full-time job, he signed on for a role as a pimp in a daytime soap opera. When the patience of his employer ran out, he would, within a short period, find work elsewhere. His abilities were not unique, however; attractive young men came along who could do very little with just as much facility. He ran through jobs in music, publishing, advertising. I'd always thought it surprising that he didn't drift off to Hollywood, where men whose talents were even more amorphous had been known to flourish.

The opportunities petered out eventually – he had developed a reputation – and I began to feel some pressure from him to do something about it, almost as if he were my responsibility. I loaned – or gave – him money, which was annoying but easy enough. And I manufactured some work by paying him to translate French plays, which he did with some skill. But obviously, I was not one of the rich and powerful men to whom he had always been able to attach himself. This not only disappointed but irritated him. It was a relief to me when Sergei Volkov came into his life.

He was a huge man in both size and vision who had built a fortune in real estate in the Far West. He had also written an opera that was performed in Seattle and a sprawling novel of the

Ukraine that had more merit than the criticisms let on. Feeling hemmed in, socially and artistically, he had moved to Manhattan to establish himself as a figure in East Coast culture. With his unfailing antennae, Beau had managed to meet him and to get us invited to a party Volkov was giving in celebration of his acquisition of a major art gallery in Soho.

It wasn't that we did much once we were there, but I have a picture of us not so much entering as sweeping into Volkov's lavish downtown penthouse, and of our flamboyant arrival catching the eye of the industrialist. Halfway along in the festivities, in a swirl of vodka and caviar, Volkov made a slighting comment about a play I had written. ("It has no center. . . .") When I took offense, a cry went up from his stunning wife who produced a pair of Tsarist sabres, handing one to each of us and encouraging us to use them. When a circle of guests formed around us, the host and I began to lunge at one another with the priceless weapons. The mood was playful – we both had a sense of theatre – but there was the chance of a dangerous escalation. Wondering how to disengage myself gracefully, I looked at Beau for some help – he knew Volkov, I didn't – but characteristically, his eyes were elsewhere. I eventually managed to withdraw and to leave the party alone and without apparent injury. When I last saw Beau, he was chatting with the Volkovs. As I prepared for bed, I noticed a perfect ring of bite marks on my shoulders. Thinking back, I recalled that Volkov had sunk his teeth into me at the door in what I thought of at the time as a show of Slavic camaraderie. To be on the safe side, I had myself treated with a tetanus shot at the emergency room of Lenox Hill Hospital, which was inconveniencing. But there was comfort in knowing that the weight of responsibility I felt for Beau had passed to another.

With Beau more or less accounted for, I continued along on a pleasant and purposeless path, contriving to have Hollywood pick up the bills for my wastrel life. Somewhere along the line, the notion took root in this country that Hollywood corrupts writers. My career is living proof that the reverse is true. I found more gentlemen in Hollywood than I did in theatre and publishing, and the West Coast variety of scoundrel had at least some size and panache. It's unlikely that I would have written *Anna Karenina* if I had stayed away from Warner Brothers.

My slender responsibilities as a film person enabled me to continue living in Manhattan. A rough goal was to stumble into a commercial success or two, dissolve and show up as an aging roué, entertaining the local shopgirls on the patio of a villa in the South of France. David Niven, had the poor man lived, would have been perfect for the role. And then one Sunday night, a time I generally reserve for sober introspection, I attended a worthy but numbingly boring documentary on the disadvantaged of Guatemala and met Helen. Warm green eyes, a wink and a chuckle and there, with no sense of loss whatever, went the South of France. She gave up her apartment, moved into mine and we divided our time between the city and a cottage we bought together on Morris Island. Part of her enormous appeal was that she was not writing a screenplay.

I saw Beau from time to time, clearing people out of Volkov's path at various restaurants and functions. He waved at me once as if he were a national politician and I was someone he vaguely recalled as having supported him at the grass roots level. Volkov had given him an office, several secretaries and a handsome budget to develop books and films related to Beau's favorite themes. I sensed trouble ahead when he called to tell me the ones he had chosen. I had once worked for a shrewd publisher who kept a list posted on his office wall of editorial subjects that were never to be presented to him since he considered them to be commercially ruinous. Beau had selected three of them. Months later, handsomely embossed but unsold volumes dealing with bullfighting and the I.R.A began to pile up in Volkov's warehouse. Not too long afterward, McMartin told me he had attended the screening of a Volkov/LeVyne film that dealt with log-rolling in the State of Washington. ("It did not go well.")

McMartin and I joined Beau one night at *Wally and Joseph's* Restaurant on West Forty-Ninth Street. He was in a despondent mood and reported that he and Volkov had parted company.

"I should have stuck with you, Cliff," he said, as if the Russian and I had waged a furious struggle for his services.

For most of the evening, he carried on a dark conversation with himself, breaking out of it now and then to rattle off the names of writers whose careers he felt were on the wane.

"To think," he said, at a later point, "that this could have happened to the great Beau LeVyne. . . ."

In an aside to me, McMartin asked, with genuine curiosity: "Why is it the *great* Beau LeVyne?"

In the men's room, as Beau and I washed up, he carried on about Volkov's treachery and broken promises. When I started for the door, he stepped in front of me, sealing us off for the moment in a fluorescent capsule of tile and concrete. I had seen the look of hatred on his face before, but it had never been directed at me.

"You're in my way, Beau," I said, with forced equanimity.

After a moment or two in which the air was murderous, he said "Sorry," as if he had accidentally sipped my drink. Then he stepped aside.

He entered into a dark phase after the Volkov experience. I learned from McMartin that he had begun to collect debts for a shylock whose specialization was lending money to writers and artists who were down on their luck. This, of course, assured him of a large and steady clientele. McMartin, an unlikely gambler, considering his slim earnings as a critic, had fallen behind in some payments and Beau had been assigned his case for collection. After a single visit to the critic proved unproductive, Beau made threatening calls to McMartin's mother in a nursing home. When I mentioned this to Beau at some later point, he shook his head in awe – and admiration.

"Cliff, you've completely missed the point. It was McMartin who called *my* mother in a nursing home."

Beau disappeared for awhile, during which time I received a card from him in Tangiers, saying he had been doing some research in the area. Soon afterward, he dropped round to our apartment to meet Helen and left after a short visit. I found a rectangular-shaped gift package on the dining room table, which I took to be a record album. It turned out to be a block of hashish, so exquisitely chiseled it might have passed for a work of art. I'm not a stranger to drugs, but as it happened, he had not picked one of my favorites. Still, it seemed a pity to waste it. I tried to make a gift of it to a street friend of mine whose permanent headquarters is an alleyway in the East Nineties.

"That's all very fine," said Spofford, after listening to me sing the praises of the exotic substance, "but I sure could use a little blow."

Helen and I began to spend most of our time on Morris Island, losing track not only of Beau but of the city as well. McMartin told me Beau had been seen around town with a man in a camouflage suit who literally threw money in every direction, fondled women indiscriminately and tossed balls of cocaine to the fish in the open tank of a Chinese restaurant on Mott Street. Soon afterward, I saw an item in the newspaper saying that Beau and his companion had been arrested and indicted on two counts of running guns and selling cocaine.

Literary friends gathered round after he had been released on bail. I was invited to a party that had been given to boost his spirits. He seemed peaceful and resigned as if some troublesome burden he carried had finally been removed. And he appeared mildly to enjoy the celebrity that had been conferred upon him. He regaled the group with stories of his incarceration at the Manhattan correctional facility, the intolerable food, the nights sleeping on the floor alongside AIDS victims. Listening to him, you would have thought he had gotten himself arrested and was off to prison on behalf of the literary community – so that he could report back on what it was like.

"My God," McMartin said to him, "you're the only one here who's actually *done* something."

The arrest seemed to draw him closer to Heidi. They joined us at the beach for dinner at our cottage. Beau was solicitous to his wife and she appeared to welcome his new concern for her. They seemed the very model of a civilized '80s couple. I envisioned future dinners for the four of us around the fire. Late in the evening, he took me aside and showed me a treatment he had written for a proposed film to be called "Bills." I glanced at it and saw that it began with a former athlete and Ivy League star disgustedly throwing his mail up in the air and saying, "Bills, bills, bills."

In the next scene, he is in Tangiers, flagging down from the hills a truck carrying a ton of hashish and a shipment of weapons. I suggested that the character and his motivation might be fleshed out a bit, but he disagreed and asked me to help him sell it to a studio. I made an attempt to do this, but without conviction or success.

Later, when I remarked to Helen on Beau's new closeness to his wife, her response was succinct.

"That woman hates that man."

Heidi filed for divorce the following week. Soon afterward, I received a call from Beau that seemed to be coming from a phone booth on the street.

"I have a little cupcake in the car," he said, "and I need some 'lady.'"

He whispered the last word, which of course was a code name for cocaine, one that was already out of vogue. I had taken the second of two scotches I allot myself during the televised seven o'clock news. Had I started on a third, I might have given him the number of an actor I know who supplements his modest income by doing voice-overs and selling small amounts of cocaine. As it was, I said it had been years since I'd had any interest in drugs.

"I'm afraid I can't help you."

"You're better off," he said glumly and hung up.

It hardly needs to be pointed out that he had been asked to cast around for dealers in exchange for a reduction of his sentence. I like to think not, but with the reality of a long prison sentence staring me in the face, I might have done the same.

McMartin reported that Beau was wearing a wire, but that I was not to be concerned.

"When it's functioning, he's going to wink broadly to alert unsuspecting friends."

It's easy to conclude that normal life ends once you've agreed to be rigged up that way, that it's a kind of castration and that only impotence can follow. I don't feel that applied in Beau's case. I can see him making a small adjustment in his private rudderless code and turning it into a feat of daring, along with gun-running and shooting the rapids, one that would earn him the awed respect of his new friends in law enforcement.

I could imagine him saying with boyish delight: "They couldn't get over it, Cliff. They'd never *seen* anyone go into the places I've gone with that wire. You have no *idea* of the people I have on tape."

I stayed away from Beau while his trial was pending since I felt I knew the way his mind worked. I sensed that he resented my freedom and felt it was unfair somehow that I had not been arrested with him.

"He carries a gun now," McMartin told me.

I could picture a scenario in which Beau would create an incident, and the two of us would end up being slaughtered side by side. He was found guilty and given a three-year sentence which seemed harsh for a first offense. There was a feeling that the expensive corporate suits he wore, the Princeton background and the letters of support that came in from luminaries had somehow worked against him.

I corresponded with Beau when he was in prison. His letters were great sheaf-like affairs in which he dwelled on familiar prison themes – the human spirit was indomitable . . . mere walls could not contain an individual . . . wasn't life itself a prison? Genet was quoted liberally. Apart from sections thrown over to Heidi's treachery, the letters seemed to be written for posterity rather than to me. And I had a sense that copies were being mailed off to others. I kept my replies short and sweet, attempting to cheer him up with items about mutual friends who had fallen low. What could I say to him? Chin up? This too shall pass? It was awful, if inevitable that he had ended up in jail and that's all there was to it. Only McMartin, with his great heart, made the long railroad journey to visit him. He reported only that Beau looked fit, and complained that he was not receiving enough magazines.

The years slipped by for me if not for Beau. I did some serviceable scripts in Hollywood. A lame effort became a hit. Helen gave birth to Derrick and it occurred to me that Beau would be envious since he had always wanted a son. After his release from prison, a party was given in his honor in which he doled out prison stories. McMartin said he was saving the best for a planned memoir. Beau then slipped off to Morris Island. I put off seeing him, not knowing what he would be like after his incarceration. I had been reading a novel by Naguib Mahfouz in which the main character eerily leaves prison and sets about to kill his wife and best friend. But it seemed cowardly to keep ducking my old friend. McMartin, with two infants of his own, had had him over for dinner without incident.

I finally agreed to meet Beau at a steak restaurant which is located on a bluff within walking distance of his beach house. It is a big and draughty place that does a brisk business during the summer months and then tails off predictably in the off-season. We had met there before and enjoyed having it virtually to ourselves in December and January. When he entered the restaurant I saw that any fears I had of him were groundless. He wore a denim jacket and seemed compact and strong, but he had aged dramatically. His eyes were watery and subdued as if he had undergone a religious conversion. Obviously, he had left something behind in prison. The net effect was heart-breaking.

As was his habit, he ordered his steak raw, not rare, the only one I'd ever known to do so. Adhering to a tradition of ours, I asked for the Steak à la Stone (sliced beef on a bed of soft onions and peppers) a dish that had first been prepared for me by Heidi. In the past, whenever I placed this order at a restaurant, Beau would call out to the waiter: "The way Heidi LeVyne makes it" and I would laugh, which delighted him since he was unsure of himself as a wit. But on this occasion, he let the waiter go without comment. He said little about prison life. His only friends had been the black inmates. He had lost an inch in height. We talked a bit about past adventures and the women we had known, but the reminiscences were stiff and had no real flavor to them.

As near as I could piece it together, he spent his days at the beach working out in the morning and doing spiritless jobs around the house; at night he fought for sleep. He seemed unable to come to grips with the reality that Heidi (who had left him) and his two daughters (fully grown and married) and his dog (dead for several years) had not all been waiting for him at the house upon his release from prison. On this subject, he was delusionary.

"If I had Helen," he said, halfway along in the evening, "it would have all been different."

The comment was unusual in that he hadn't seemed to notice my wife. This is not easy to say, but Helen is a plain-looking woman. It surprised me that the qualities I found appealing in her – the twinkle and the strength and the loyalty – were apparent to others. It occurred to me when he made the remark – and not without some shitty satisfaction – that over the years our positions had become reversed. When we first met, he was shored up by his family and I felt I had very little. Now, unforgivably, I had Helen and Derrick and he was the one without hope. As far as he was concerned it all came down to that and he may have been right.

I saw him for dinner from time to time in the months that followed. After one such meeting, we visited a local pub, making a modest stab, I would suppose, to recapture one of our nights on the town. Quickly, I struck up a conversation with an attractive doctor who lived in Manhattan and was spending a quiet week on the island. While not entirely ruling her out as a candidate for myself, I tried to steer her around to Beau, who was available. She knew nothing of the stay in prison, but obviously saw something in him that I did not. Gathering up her things, she left quickly.

Despite the sad content of the evenings, they were pleasing to me; unlike Helen, who had fallen in with a group of young mothers, I had not made any friends on the island.

"Such is the state of my life that the only one I look forward to having dinner with is Beau LeVyne."

I said this to McMartin, expecting him to laugh, but he had become a moral rock and only stared at me judgmentally.

Beau called one morning and said he had a present for me.

"Can we have dinner tonight so I can give it to you?"

It was short notice, and I had other plans, but I picked up some urgency in his voice, and I agreed to meet him. Then, too, I have a weakness for presents and was curious to see what he had picked out for me. He limped noticeably when he came into the restaurant; I asked him what was wrong. He said that he had developed a chronic hip injury in prison and had been advised to undergo surgery. It was an option he waved off as being pointless. He had learned that he was about to lose the beach house in the divorce settlement – which would leave him without a place to live and he had taken this badly. I had been having some trouble of my own at home and saw this situation as an opportunity. He was a relatively young man – just turned fifty.

"Why not just pick up stakes," I said, "start over in a new place – Paris or Portugal . . . or Hong Kong."

There was the parole limitation, but why couldn't he just disappear and create a new identity? There were friends, myself included, who would give him money to do so. I felt that if I could do such a thing, why not Beau? But whatever I said disappeared into blank eyes and a head that suddenly seemed made of straw.

Toward the end of our dinner, he brought out the present. It was an embossed T-shirt given to cast members of a play I'd written many years before. They had formed a Broadway Show League softball team. I had turned up for the game only to find Beau, playing my position at third base. I didn't understand what he was doing there – he had no connection with the show – but he had the facility of doing that, simply showing up in similar situations. As a result, I'd had to spend the afternoon at *second* base, off-balance, able to field the ball but clumsy in making the throw to first base. I was annoyed at the time and wondered why he had done that. I had written the play, why couldn't I play my position? But that, of course, was the point. I had the play, I didn't need the position.

I thanked Beau for the shirt, which I suspected hadn't been laundered, and hugged him in the parking lot, continuing – and for some reason with mounting alarm – to suggest faraway places for him to go, ones without extradition treaties. When I had run out of ideas, he got behind the wheel of his battered Alfa Romeo sports car and drove off. A waitress, who was finishing her shift, watched him drive off.

She said: "That's the loveliest car I've ever seen."

McMartin called several weeks later to say that Beau had committed suicide; to do so, he had rigged up a smothering contraption in his basement.

"It's something he learned in prison," said McMartin.

I can't say that I was shocked, but I was surprised. No matter what the signs, you don't expect someone in decent health to leave the party when it's in full swing. But of course for Beau there had never been a party.

There was a small ceremony in a nondescript church on Morris Island. A few, but not many of his literary friends attended. The church was filled for the most part with young local couples. Beau had worked with them as an athletic coach in the community, leaving one to wonder why he wouldn't have done more of that instead of attaching himself to celebrated writers.

McMartin was the only speaker. An authority on deconstructionist criticism and a man who had interpreted the most arcane of literary works, he struggled with his remarks and finally threw up his hands.

"I did not understand Beau LeVyne."

When the ceremony had ended, McMartin and I watched the pretty girls as they left the church. I tried to lighten the atmosphere.

"Is it bad form," I asked, "to cruise a friend's wake?"

He gave me one of his gray looks and I decided never again to tell him any jokes.

A few of us trooped off to the island pub. When we had ordered drinks, a bearded public relations man I'd never thought of as being insightful said, with regard to Beau's literary friendships: "He tasted the lion's heart and thought he would become the lion."

The supermarket boy who had replaced me in the infamous volleyball game was there.

"It took a lot of balls to do what Mr. LeVyne did," he said.

Taking the party line, I said it took more courage not to do what he did – but I knew what he meant.

An instantly unpleasant man who had gone to school with Beau joined us and said that Beau had registered at Princeton as Benny Levine.

"His father was a racing tout at Aqueduct."

And then the man left, as if his sole purpose in being there was to make this announcement. I thought he might have something to say about the perfect little story Beau had published – but the writing of it was to remain a mystery.

The bartender, who looked like a boy but turned out to be a girl, said that Beau had been to the pub on a few occasions.

"What was your impression of him?" McMartin asked.

"He was very nice," she said, and then added what to me was the saddest note of all. "He asked me to go to a movie."

Could any of us have saved him? (And I'm aware here that I've conveniently made us into a group.) He gave off enough signals; yet none of us responded. What would it have required? Moving in with him? Holding his hand? Staying with him until he got to another place? In that arrangement he might have continued on indefinitely. There isn't a doubt in my mind that he would have done this much for any one of us. If nothing else, it would have given him an activity. But he had time on his hands; we were occupied and turned away. Was it that he had outlived his usefulness? That he was glum and played out and had lost his entertainment value?

Was it a relief to have him out of the way?

If his intention was to make us feel his absence, he succeeded brilliantly. Time and again, I feel myself being tugged in the direction of that cruel stretch of beach in front of Beau's cottage. I've driven past it more than once, thinking we did have some fun.

Helen and I had dinner at the steak house one night. It was her idea. She doesn't care much for meat, but her young mothers had told her that the fries were exceptional – and she was anxious to try them. There was a great fire going and it was just us and a local real estate man I knew who ate his dinner at a corner table, bitter and alone. Helen and I caught up on the previous week and talked about everything but Beau. It wasn't until I got behind the wheel and we had started back that I became emotional and pulled over to the side of the road. This had the advantage of showing my wife that I was a caring person after all; my reward was a kiss and an arm around my shoulder.

"You really loved him, didn't you."

"I wouldn't go that far," I said, although I no longer feared the word. "But I certainly do miss the sonofabitch."

Acknowledgments

"The Secret Man" and "Fit As a Fiddle" were published in *Tri-Quarterly*. "The Convert," "Neck and Neck" and "The Reversal" in *The Antioch Review*. "An Affair," "Three Balconies," and "A Pebble In His Shoe" in *Playboy*. "The Investigative Reporter," "I Don't Want Her, You Can Have Her," "Mr. Wimbledon," and "Knee-socks" in *Hampton Shorts Magazine*. "Protect Yourself At All Times" in *The Magazine of Fantasy and Science Fiction*. "Joined at the Hip" in *Murdaland*.